TALES GUARANTEED TO

Good Tales

To Kris
Hope you enjoy
the read.
Louie
Sept 2014

Louis Winslow

Outskirts Press, Inc.
Denver, Colorado

Good Tales
All Rights Reserved.
Copyright © 2011 Louis Winslow
v2.0

Cover Photo © 2011 JupiterImages Corporation. All rights reserved - used with permission.

Outskirts Press, Inc.
http://www.outskirtspress.com

ISBN: 978-1-4327-7508-7

Outskirts Press and the "OP" logo are trademarks belonging to Outskirts Press, Inc.

PRINTED IN THE UNITED STATES OF AMERICA

Table of Contents

Bad Seed...1

Guilt 9

Accused.. 19

Twist of Fate 29

A Love Square 37

"Ambush"... 47

Artificial 55

Charade.. 62

War Memorial....................................... 72

Lotto 81

Choices 89

Accidental Christmas Meal...................... 97

Donation 102

Satan 110

The Loop...117

The Crossing 123

Mixed-breed...129

Triathlon 140

Woody 148

Trophy 157

Bad Seed

The man gripped the chain tightly with his stained yellow fingers, while Jake strained against it. Nauseated, the man burped, and a strong smell of beer escaped his lips. A discarded two-by-four lay in his path; Jake lunged and dragged him over it. The man stumbled and cursed, not seeing the board because of his protruding belly.

The pockets of the man's jeans bulged from the bills he had stuffed into them after the fight, and he patted them with his free hand and smiled. "We did all right, Jake. I sure hope you can fight one more time."

When they reached the door of the shed, Jake sat and whined, staring at his master with large amber eyes. A massive pit bull with the coloring of an aquatic mud puppy, he thumped his tail and scratched at the door. His hide had numerous scabs. A jagged cut went from the base of his neck and disappeared under his belly. Crudely sewn up, it oozed a mixture of blood and clear fluid. The man opened the shed door and Jake lunged, jerking the man's arm, causing him to jerk back. "Jesus Christ, Jake, I'll get your food as quick as I can."

The man approached the eye bolt sticking out of the center of the cement floor. Just as he reached to attach the chain's snap to it, his face contorted, he dropped the chain, and he clawed at his chest. Toppling to the cement, his body bounced, and his face landed with a loud smack. The shed became quiet except for the sounds of Jake's labored breathing. After a short wait, the dog approached his prone master and sniffed at his face, but the man did not respond. Jake opened his mouth, saliva drooled onto the man's nostrils, and he licked his master's forehead and eyes. The saliva clung to the end of the nose but did not bubble or move. Jake lay down near the corpse and pushed up against it. When he had waited for his master to get up for over six hours, hunger pangs got the better of him, and he trotted out the open door and into the bright sunshine of morning.

Jake headed for the town which lay a mile in the distance. As he padded along the shoulder of the road, the trailing chain raised little dust clouds. His stomach growled and his throat hurt. After a few minutes of trotting, his tongue hung out, and his ribs throbbed and sent little messages of pain to his brain every time a foot touched down. When he had gone half-a-mile, he came to a major road, and without looking, started across. Tires squealed and a horn sounded so Jake broke into a run. A car's right front tire narrowly missed him, and the driver rolled down the window and yelled, "You Goddamn mangy mutt, get out of the way."

A half-an-hour later, he entered a residential section and spotted a blue plastic pool full of water in a backyard. He ran over to it, plunged his muzzle in, lapping up the water, its coolness soothing his raw throat and quenching his thirst. A few lots down, a door opened and a black Lab emerged. A scent wafted on the breeze. Jake lifted his head, sniffed the tantalizing odor, spied the Lab, and headed directly for it. As Jake approached the dog, it hunkered down and wagged its tail. He stuck his muzzle up the bitch's rear end and took a deep breath; his heart sped up as he breathed in the delicious scent. His tail looked like a windshield wiper put on an insane speed, and after a couple of minutes, he mounted her. Afterward, he left the bitch; she trotted after him for a ways, but he turned and growled. The bitch hesitated, turned, and went back home.

He trotted further down the tree lined street going another fourteen blocks before he spotted a golden retriever playing with a Frisbee. It saw him and ran to the edge of its yard and barked. Jake bolted forward, the chain bumping and clanging behind him. The golden retriever tried to turn away when Jake slammed into it. He opened his jaws, exposing his large yellowed teeth, and clamped onto the other dog's neck. It attempted to drag him across the yard, but he held on and shook his head back and forth. They both toppled to the ground and rolled in the grass. The other dog struggled, trying to get up, but Jake held on and forced his teeth deeper. The other dog went limp just as the door of the house burst open and a man came out with a shotgun in his hands. Jake didn't let go even when the cold barrel of the gun was thrust into his ear. A blast came and lightning pain surged through his brain, and then all went black.

Tom O'Brien, dressed in his pin stripped suit, looked at the swollen belly of his Lab Molly five weeks later, and nodded to his wife, Alice. "I think she is pregnant. Can you take her into Doc Connell just to make sure?"

"Sure. Is the kennel in the back of the station wagon?"

Tom scratched his head. "Yeah, it is. I wonder who the father is. I wanted to breed her with Jerry's dog, but I guess I won't be able to now."

Four weeks later, Molly had a litter of seven puppies; four males and three females. Alice came into the room where the dogs lay in a box with blankets and looked at the squirming animals. Six of the puppies were coal black like their mother, but one had an ugly mottled coat and a shortened muzzle.

A month later, Alice looked at her husband while he sat eating his breakfast. "You can take the puppies in for their four week shots."

She held the mottled male in her hands, and it squirmed trying to lick her face. She laughed. "This one is so ugly he is cute."

Its little pink tongue lapped against her face, and she brought the puppy to her cheek and hugged it. Her curly dark hair tickled the dog's nose and it sneezed. Alice kissed its little snooze. "My goodness, quite a loud sound for a little puppy."

Later that day, Doc Connell, an older man with grizzled, white hair, sad, blue eyes, and large, but gentle hands, had just finished giving the last puppy its shot.

"What kind of dog do you think the sire was, Doc?"

Doc Connell picked up the mottled male. It wiggled and squirmed trying to get out of his grasp and nipped at his hand. Connell set the puppy down. "If I were to guess, I'd say it was a pit bull. What are you going to do with them?"

"I probably can't get any money for them, so I will just give them away."

Connell frowned. "If I'm right about the pit bull you might want to consider destroying them. I wouldn't take a chance since the sire of these puppies may have had bad genes."

Tom shook his head. "Ah come on, Doc. If you treat a dog well, it won't be a problem. Anyway, Alice would never forgive me if I had these puppies put down."

A month later, all the puppies were gone except for the mottled male. When the phone rang, Alice picked it up.

"The O'Brien's."

"Hello. This is Margaret James. Are you the people who have the Lab mixed puppies to give away?"

"Yes, but we only have one left."

"Can I and my kids come over to see it?"

"Sure. What time do you think you'll be over?"

"In a couple of hours. How do we get to your place?"

A while later the doorbell rang, Alice went to their entrance, and opened the door. Standing there was a petite blond woman with huge blue eyes along with a young boy wearing dirty sneakers and a torn Twin's jersey. A small girl with double braids and dressed in a pink top and jeans fidgeted by the woman's side.

"Mrs. O'Brien."

Alice smiled. "Yes, you must be Margaret. Please come in. I suppose you are here about the puppy."

The little girl clapped her hands and grinned. "We sure are. Can we see it?"

"You sure can. Molly and the puppy are out back. What are your names?"

"I'm Jennifer and my brother's name is Peter, but everybody calls him Shag."

She motioned for them to follow her and said, "My name is Alice."

They stepped out into the backyard which had a fence all around it. Molly and the puppy were playing along the fence at the rear of the property. Jennifer ran over to the puppy and picked him up. The dog wiggled free from her grasp, fell, and ran back to Molly. Jennifer chased after it, and when she caught it, she stroked its head. "Can we get him, please, Mom?"

Margaret said to Alice, "I have been divorced for over a year. The kids are having a bad time and I thought a dog may help."

"I agree. A dog gives unconditional love."

Margaret turned to her daughter and gave thumbs up. Peter grinned, ran over to Jennifer and petted the puppy. It turned its head and nipped at his hand. Peter jerked his hand away "Ouch, that hurts."

Alice scowled. "Tell him bad dog when he does that. What are you going to name him?"

Jennifer jumped up and down, her eyes large in her freckled face.

"Let's call him Cuddles."

Cuddles grew rapidly; he had a voracious appetite and wolfed down any food put into his bowl. Every day Jennifer and Peter could not wait to get home from school so they could play with him.

Margaret stared at the muddy tracks on her living room rug and frowned. If they could confine Cuddles to the kitchen her house work would be much easier. Jennifer came into the kitchen, and pointed at Cuddles who lay on the floor, his feet moving in the air. As they watched he gave a short bark. "Please, Mom. Can't Cuddles sleep with me?"

"Absolutely not."

Later that night, when Margaret got up to go to the bathroom, she looked in each of the kid's bedroom. When she looked in on Jennifer, she saw Cuddles lying with his muzzle up against Jennifer's cheek. Her little girl's arm lay across the dog's neck, and as she watched, the dog stuck its tongue out and started licking Jennifer's face. Margaret resisted smiling, her lips twitching at the corners of her mouth, but then she gave in and smiled. She thought the dog really did live up to his name.

Three months later Margaret was vacuuming here living room for the umpteenth time. She had given up about where Cuddles stayed and slept. Margaret flicked off the switch on the vacuum, and looked out into the backyard. She smiled when she heard sounds of giggling and squealing as she watched Cuddles chase the kids around their lot. After a few minutes she sighed, turned the vacuum back on, and resumed her cleaning. It always amazed her how quickly Cuddles got the rug dirty. A few minutes later Peter grabbed her by the hand and tugged. She turned and looked at his tear stained face, his eyes wild. "Momma, come quick. Cuddles is fighting another dog."

Margaret looked out the window. On her right she saw a heavyset woman holding a broken lead, and as Margaret watched, the woman yelled, "Duke!" In the back of the yard, Cuddles and a black dog circled each other while Jennifer danced around them. Margaret screamed, "Oh my God", ran over to the patio door, jerked it open, and charged across the lawn. The black dog lunged and grabbed Cuddles by the throat. They both went down, the black dog shook its head, and blood gushed from Cuddle's throat. Jennifer grabbed the left hind leg of the black dog and pulled. Before Margaret could get there, the monster turned on Jennifer, its bloody jaws snapping. It lunged and attacked. Jennifer sprawled and squealed as the thing attacked her face. Margaret finally reached them and grasped the tail of the black dog. Adrenaline kicked in as she jerked it with all her might. The animal spun around, its lips curled back, and it charged. Her own scream echoed in her ears as she ran. She tripped on something and went down hard, seeing stars as her chin hit the ground. The metallic taste of blood filled her mouth as her punctured tongue sent pain shooting to her brain. The dog was on her and tried to grab her by the throat. She twisted away and punched it in the snout. It backed off; seeming confused, but then came at her again. Out of the corner of her eye she saw Peter's bat. Snatching it up, she hit the dog as hard as she could in the head. The blow landed with a satisfying thud, pain shot up her wrist, and the dog went down. She grasped the bat with two hands, and before the monster could get up, she walloped it. Hate charged through her like heat lightning in a roiling summer storm, and she continued to whack the animal. Someone kept yelling, "Stop, stop, you are killing my dog."

Exhausted, she finally quit; tears streamed down her face, and her breaths came in ragged gasps. Shoving the woman out of the way, she ran over to Jennifer. Margaret looked at her baby's face. A lifeless, bloody, mass stared back at her. Margaret screamed like a wounded animal, and collapsed

Pixie strained against the chain. Unlike Duke and Cuddles, her litter mates, she had Molly's smaller size. However, she had Jake and Duke's temperament in spades. Her handler unsnapped her chain, and she charged across the ring, slamming into the other dog.

Guilt

George watched Rhonda walk toward the entrance doors. Her butt swayed from side to side as she oozed sexuality from every point of her curvaceous body. In his mind a war waged, and before she reached the doors he decided and said, "Rhonda, wait. I want to talk about your application to college. "

As he said this his hand went to the cross dangling from a chain around his neck and he caressed its cool, smooth surface.

Rhonda turned and said, "Yes, Reverend Thiesen, what about it?"

The first meeting of Youth Group had just finished. George first spied Rhonda at fourteen when she came for confirmation classes. God, even at that age she had aroused him. Now a senior, she would turn eighteen in three months. He overheard the girls around Rhonda talking about their boyfriends and learned she recently broke-up with hers.

"What school are you planning on attending?"

His wife and George didn't have any children after fifteen years of marriage. They tried but when tested he learned that he had a low sperm count. The unsympathetic ape of a doctor told him he COULD get his wife pregnant but the probability was low.

"I plan on going to North Central Illinois."

Rhonda, a brilliant student as well as a sexual nymph, looked him straight in the eyes as she said this and an electrical charge raced through George as he saw her pupils dilate.

"I would like to write you a recommendation. You know, I graduated from there and my word carries some weight. I am a big alumni contributor. Let's go to my office and we will discuss it."

When they got there, George ushered her inside and shut the door, locking it with an audible click. At the sound Rhonda turned and giggled.

"Before we discuss the recommendation I'd like you to see something."

George went over to the bookshelf and took down a leather bound bible and set it on his desk.

"This is beautiful. Where did you get it?" Rhonda ran her fingers over the cover and took a deep breath. "I love the smell of leather."

"Open it to Second Samuel, chapter eleven, and read what it says in the beginning verses."

Rhonda opened the book and leaning over, began reading. George came up behind her and pressed his body against her.

She stopped reading and turning around, smiled and said, "I think I know what you want Reverend Thiesen. Do you think I'm as desirable as Bathsheba?"

Rhonda fell to her knees, unzipped his fly, and grasped him, squeezing his member. He managed to croak, "Call me George."

Afterward she did a double strip tease throwing both their clothes around his office. He took her on his couch; his tongue tingled with the delicious taste of her. Both she and he became covered in a thin layer of sweat, and they cried out and moaned as they climaxed together. As they untangled, Rhonda took the cross in her hand and said, "Where did you get this?"

"My parents gave it to me when I graduated from seminary."

After Rhonda left, George thought about what happened. He knew he would have to be careful since he didn't what to jeopardize his career. Just last week Wilson talked to him about trying for a head minister position.

"You are a dynamic youth leader, George. I think you would make a fantastic head minister at a prestigious church. I would be happy to write you a recommendation."

As he thought about this, George caressed his cross and smiled remembering what he told Rhonda. Jean Marie gave it to him their senior year of high school. Jean Marie, the best lay he'd ever had took up with a football player the first year of college, the cunt. They were to be married after graduating. Rhonda reminded George of her, maybe that is why he'd seduced her.

Todd walked through the lightening woods; before he reached his spot a gobble rang out from the valley below. His pulse ticked up a notch and he smiled. His favorite season, spring, had arrived. It gave him the opportunity to hunt wild turkey which he thoroughly enjoyed. In the predawn darkness he set up on the edge of a clearing where he found many signs. The woods filled with gobbling, but later the toms quit and the day became warm. It was very pleasant, but not good hunting. He hoped at least one tom would still be seeking an amorous hen.

Low blossoms of the tree dangled right before his face, and a Ruby Throated humming bird greedily sucked nectar from the flowers. Its wings buzzed as it hovered inches from him. He looked at its small beady eye through his mesh mask as it moved forward and backwards, flitting from flower to flower. Dressed in complete camouflage, he sat watching the bird.

His butt ached; he shifted on his cushion trying to get comfortable. He heard something approaching and froze. Leaves rustled and he looked to the opposite side of the clearing and saw a girl enter the meadow carrying a blanket. It was Rhonda, his neighbor Tom's daughter. She walked within a few feet of him and spread the blanket on the ground. Todd remembered watching her as she grew up. His house sat on the edge of a park and he enjoyed seeing the kids play ball. Rhonda, a Tomboy, could play with the best of them and at twelve years old she dominated the diamond. When he came home from work one July day, he discovered his back bedroom window broken. While examining it, he found a softball lying underneath it.

"Mr. Sullivan?"

Todd turned and saw Rhonda. She shifted from foot to foot and tugged at her dirty tee shirt.

"Yes."

"I broke your window this afternoon."

"Wow, you really connected."

"I'll pay for it."

"Don't worry about the money, I'll take it into Ace and have the pane replaced."

"Are you sure?"

"Yeah, I'm sure. Thanks for telling me about it."

Rhonda smiled and turning around, skipped home.

When grades came out for junior high he noted she made the honor-roll. Now a senior she had developed into a beautiful girl and moved lasciviously without trying. Many times when Tom mowed his yard, she also came out to mow. She would bend down to start her dad's mower, her breasts straining against the cloth of her halter as she tugged the starter cord. She usually wore short shorts which exposed her long smooth legs. Curvaceous, she did not have an angular spot on her entire body. Guilt flooded him as he watched her, and he chastised himself for being a dirty old man.

Rhonda sat down and looked toward the other side of the glen. After a short time Todd heard someone approaching. A man entered the clearing and walked over to Rhonda. When he reached her, she got up and he embraced her. Their lips crushed together. They fell on top of the blanket and she moaned as they undressed each other. Todd smelled Rhonda's musk. He couldn't believe it, a porno flick flashed through his mind as he watched. His face became hot and his breathing increased in tempo.

It seemed to go on for an eternity. Todd had no feeling in his left leg and his ass hurt. Sweat beaded on his forehead and rivulets formed, he blinked as sweat stung his eyes. He wanted to get up and move around but he didn't dare.

They finally sat up and started dressing. Todd studied the man. He appeared about forty, wore a wedding ring, and had a muscular build with a full head of wavy black hair. Todd noticed tinges of gray as the man turned his head. His hooded eyelids accentuated his blue eyes. A smile played across his wide sensual mouth.

"I love you, George."

"I love you too. Can you get away next Thursday?"

George turned and stared at Todd. Todd's chest constricted and he held his breath. His pulse pounded in his ears. Dropping his gaze, he looked at the dead leaves scattered on the ground. After a long time George turned back to Rhonda.

"What is the matter? Did you see something?"

"It must be my imagination; it felt like someone staring at us. How about next Thursday?"

"You know I can't resist you. Can we go someplace and eat?"

"Maybe, but baby you know we have to be very careful."

George grabbed her and they started kissing again. Todd watched their lips lock together; their mouths opened and closed as their heads moved about. He thought they were going to lie back down and he had to stifle a yell.

"I have to leave, baby." George released her.

"Do you have to go?"

"Yes."

He turned and walked away. When he reached the meadow's edge he turned around and took a few steps back toward Rhonda.

Todd suppressed a groan, he willed George away.

Rhonda waved, "Until next Thursday, I have to be going."

Rhonda rose to her feet, picked up the blanket, and left the way she had come.

Todd looked in George's direction, the meadow was empty. Sighing, he got to his feet and almost fell down. His legs like dead stumps; hundreds of needles stuck in them and he stumbled forward. He gritted his teeth, cursing Rhonda and George.

On Wednesday, after his turkey hunt, he read in his church bulletin the Reverend G. L. Thiesen, the youth leader at Zion's Lutheran church, would speak at their church on Sunday. Joan and Todd attended 1st Methodist.

When he and Joan got to church the parking lot was almost full. They entered the sanctuary and saw a few spaces in back. They sat down in the last pew a short time before the service started. When it came time for the sermon, Reverend Miller climbed into the pulpit and introduced the guest speaker. Reverend Thiesen sat down front so Todd couldn't see him. After the introduction, Reverend Miller climbed down and Reverend Thiesen began his ascent. When he became visible Todd's eyes popped open and he leaned forward. Reverend Thiesen was George!

George began, "As many of you know I am the youth minister at Zion's Lutheran church. My passion is ministering to young people. One of the requirements for a leader is honesty and love of young adults."

Todd gazed over the assemblage. Everyone appeared to be paying attention. Todd was dumbfounded. His armpits became wet and his forehead hot. He wanted to jump up and shout this man was a fraud. Todd squirmed, his feet rapped out a tattoo.

Joan reached over and grabbed his arm, she whispered, "What is the matter?"

George continued with his talk. "Let me assure you that I have the well-being of the youth as my top priority. Nothing matters more to me than teaching young people about morality and living a Christian life."

Todd could stand no more. He responded in a hoarse voice, "I have to go to the bathroom."

Making his way down the pew, he tried to go as fast as possible. He had to get out of here before he did something foolish. As he neared the aisle, he stepped on old Mrs. Parson's toe.

"Excuse me"

She grimaced and growled, "Can't you be a little more careful?"

He reached the end of the pew. As he left the sanctuary, he heard George say, "We have to help our youth deal with sexual problems."

The doors swung shut behind him and he could no longer hear what George said. After the service when he met Joan in the church reception room she asked him why he left.

"I felt sick and hung around the bathroom. I feel fine now."

That evening Joan talked about Reverend Thiesen and what a wonderful man he was. She knew why the youth group at Zion's Lutheran was so dynamic and growing. Joan gushed over him.

"What we need at our church is a man like Reverend Thiesen to lead our youth."

Todd could stand it no longer: All the time Joan talked about George he bit his tongue and ground his teeth.

"If you only knew, Joan."

"What do you mean?"

"Remember when I went turkey hunting a couple of weeks ago?"

"Yes, but what does that have to do with Reverend Thiesen?"

The thought flashed through Todd's mind, if I tell Joan I know she will have to blab it all over. He hesitated.

"Well, tell me."

Todd realized he wanted to tell her.

"Well, guess who I saw making love to Rhonda? The Right Reverend George L. Thiesen."

Joan's jaw opened, but no sound emerged. She finally stammered, "You must be wrong."

"I am not wrong; they were writhing around on a blanket only a few feet from me."

Todd told her what he saw in the glen. Small white spots appeared on her cheeks as her face flushed.

"Reverend Thiesen is a despicable individual. I'm going to call Reverend Wilson tomorrow and make an appointment to see him. Get up and turn off the light so we can go to sleep."

When Todd arrived home the next evening, Joan stood waiting at the door. She followed him into the kitchen.

"I had an appointment with Reverend Wilson today and told him all about Mr. Thiesen."

"What did he say?"

"Reverend Wilson said he would take care of the matter."

Shouts came from the office and then the door jerked open. George emerged white as a ghost and he stumbled, almost falling when he ran into a corner of Mildred's desk on his way out. Reverend Wilson appeared, his face flushed, and told Mildred George would be forced to resign.

"Why?"

"He and Rhonda Schroder were having an affair."

Mildred gasped and said, "Not Tom's daughter."

"Yes."

The news spread like a raging fire through Zion's and spilled out into the community.

Zion's congregation dealt with the matter, and a meeting was called. Mildred, Zion's long time secretary and a friend of Todd and Joan's, told them about it. Todd thought George should be criminally prosecuted, but her family did not want Rhonda identified. George

resigned from the ministry. At the congregational meeting he attempted to apologize for his actions. Todd and Joan attended the service
since they both came to hear what George would say.

George had lost weight and there were dark circles under his eyes.
He spoke in a low voice.

Partway through the attempted apology, his voice quavered and he
stopped, his face scrunched up, and his eyes became wet. He stared
at the ceiling. After a few minutes he descended from the pulpit and
walked down the aisle looking straight ahead. A collective murmur
swept through the congregation and people turned around to watch
as he left the church. The doors swung shut, closing with a resounding
bang.

Notes from the pipe organ reverberated through the sanctuary as
the soloist sang "Morning Has Broken." The funeral director and his
assistant wheeled the coffin down the center aisle of the church.

As it drew near Todd, the scent of flowers washed over him like
a wave breaking over a reef. Tears formed in his eyes and he com-
pressed his lips. He glanced over at Joan; her head sagged forward so
he reached over and gave her hand a squeeze. As he drew in the perfume of the flowers, he no longer sat in the pew but again sat under
the apple tree recalling what had happened.

Reverend Wilson's booming voice brought him out of his reverie
as he started the eulogy. Todd continued to stare at the casket all the
way through it.

Reverend Wilson finally finished speaking and ascended into the
pulpit. "Let us pray." Dear God, let us forgive George, we pray for him
and his wife. May they find strength and refuge in the Lord. We pray
for the family of the girl. May they find solace with You and find it in

their hearts to also forgive. In Jesus name we pray. Amen."

The pall bearers lined up on either side of the coffin. The funeral director and his assistant wheeled the casket as the soloist sang "He Lifts Me Up On Eagle's Wings." Sobbing and sniffling sounds filled the sanctuary. As the solemn group drew near, Todd saw Rhonda and George once again in the clearing. He focused on the casket with no expression, but his insides churned. He camouflaged his guilt well as the coffin glided past on its way out of the church.

On the autopsy report the medical examiner wrote, female, eighteen-years-old, for cause of death, suicide from an overdose of sleeping pills. Under pregnant it said yes, two and one half months.

Accused

"Push, Martha, push."

Martha grimaced and gritted her teeth as she arched her back and bore down. With a gush of blood the baby girl slid out into Elizabeth's hands. Puckering up, the baby began to cry.

"Good job, Martha," said Elizabeth. She held up the infant.

Martha sighed and a huge smile spread across her face.

Taking a knife, Elizabeth cut the umbilical cord and tied it. She used a warm wet cloth to wash the new born and then placed her next to Martha.

"What are you and Ned going to name her?"

Looking at her new daughter with shining eyes, Martha replied; "We plan to call her Rebecca."

"God has given you Rebecca, rejoice and dedicate her to the Lord."

Fifteen-year-old Elizabeth had helped her mother since her tenth birthday and her proficiency as a midwife and healer now rivaled her mother's.

When Elizabeth arrived home the smell of apple blossoms wafted over her and she heard the humming of bees. In this year of the Lord, 1652, they had a wondrous life in Connecticut. The woods were full of game, the soil rich, but most importantly, they could practice their religion in freedom. Her Puritan parents had arrived here in 1630; their community of Wellington had grown and now contained one thousand four hundred and twenty-three souls.

When Rebecca was two weeks old, Martha and her husband had her baptized.

Coming into the church, William walked past Elizabeth. William from Farmington, a town seven miles distant, had arrived for the christening of his newest niece. A twenty-year-old bachelor, he possessed handsome features. He smiled at Elizabeth and she looked up. She boldly held his gaze as she returned his smile. William's face burned and he averted his eyes.

After the service, William pointed to Elizabeth and asked Martha, "Who is that?"

"She is the daughter of Wellington's healer and midwife, Sarah Stewart."

"Is she married or betrothed?"

Giving William a knowing grin, Martha stated, "No."

Martha told William where the Stewarts lived and later in the day he called on them.

The next Sunday he hiked to Wellington and escorted Elizabeth to church. Thereafter, he arose early on Sunday mornings and walked to Wellington to attend services with her. Afterward, he always ate dinner with the Stewarts. Sarah, widowed for two years, enjoyed his company as much as her daughter. After eleven months, William asked Elizabeth to marry him and she accepted. They married on a blustery day in February.

"Will you William, take Elizabeth for your wife and do you promise to love, honor, and protect her as long as you both shall live, so help you God?"

"I do."

William, the town's cooper, had built a house in Farmington anticipating living there with her. When Elizabeth and he arrived, he pushed open the door and carried his new bride across the threshold. William marveled at her lightness.

Staring intently into his dark blue eyes Elizabeth said, "Will you always love and protect me, William?"

"Yes," he replied and lowered his mouth to hers. They kissed, tentatively at first, and then passionately.

At their first church service, William introduced his new bride to the congregation.

"Elizabeth is a skilled healer and has agreed to attend the sick here."

Looking out over the pews, William saw many smiles and nodding heads.

Elizabeth aided many people in Farmington during the following months. Her mother had taught her well. There were many babies to help deliver, and Elizabeth kept busy.

On a day in May, Elizabeth searched for wild strawberries three miles from town.

Her neighbors warned her about venturing too far from home. "There are wild Indians living around here. They are savages and devil worshipers. Don't go too far, Elizabeth."

She scoffed at their advice. Her mother learned about many wonderful medicinal plants and herbs from the Mohegan's. Elizabeth smiled. The breezes blowing off the western hillside brought her the scent of dogwood blossoms. She'd never picked berries in this particular spot. A small creek gurgled and flowed in the bottom of the valley and its banks were lined with willows. As she picked the luscious fruit, she started praying. "God, your earth is truly wonderful and fertile. I hope you bless William and me with a child." Looking toward the stream, Elizabeth spotted movement. Putting down her basket, she stared intently at the spot where the willows had swayed. Suddenly, a young Indian woman emerged from them only thirty yards away. She gazed around and spotted Elizabeth. Her eyes widened and she turned and started walking away.

"Wait!"

The Indian halted in midstride and spun around, facing Elizabeth.

Smiling and extending her arms, Elizabeth said, "Do you speak English?"

Nodding, the woman responded, "A little."

From that day on, Elizabeth and Running Doe became friends. Running Doe told Elizabeth she gathered the inner bark from willows along this stream. Like Elizabeth's, Running Doe's mother, a shaman, had instructed her eldest daughter in the art of healing.

"Willow bark is good for preparing a tea for fever, Elizabeth."

Running Doe and Elizabeth met often and exchanged information. They usually met near the spot they had encountered each other the first time. Running Doe had shown Elizabeth how to gather the willow bark and brew tea. With summer an illness accompanied with a high fever swept through the village. Elizabeth administered the tea to her patients and she saved a number of lives.

Now October, a pregnant Elizabeth patiently waited for Running Doe in their favorite meeting place, the valley with the creek whose banks were lined with willows. Unknown to her, Anne Wilson, the nine-year-old daughter of Elizabeth and Williams' neighbors, followed her from town. Anne liked Elizabeth, one adult who always talked to her. She wanted to find out where Elizabeth went when she ventured out in the woods. Peeking out from behind a bush, she wanted to call out to her friend, but she swallowed her words when she spied Running Doe. Her eyes became saucers and her heart thumped and beat wildly. Jumping up, she raced back toward town.

"Who is the little girl, Elizabeth?"

"What girl?"

"She just ran off behind you."

Shrugging, Elizabeth grinned and said, "Place your hands on my belly, Running Doe."

Running Doe put her palms on Elizabeth's swollen stomach. Elizabeth's abdomen jumped and Running Doe smiled.

"The Great Spirit is good to you, Elizabeth."

When Anne reached home she burst into the house. Her mother

stood cooking at the fireplace. Anne came up to her and gasped out, "Guess who I saw Elizabeth with?"

"Leave me child, don't you see I'm busy?"

"An Indian."

Spinning around, Anne's mother grabbed and shook her. "Did you say you saw Elizabeth with a heathen Indian?"

Nodding, Anne's face reddened and she started crying.

"Where?"

"Out in the woods," she wailed.

Narrowing her eyes, her mother said, "I'll have to tell Reverend Smith about this."

Two weeks later Anne lay on her bed with a fever. Her temperature dangerously high, she moaned and thrashed about as threatening monsters appeared in her dreams.

"Can you help my daughter, Elizabeth?" Anne's mother pleaded wringing her hands.

"I think I can, Penelope. I'll brew her some willow bark tea."

Holding Anne's head upright, Elizabeth got her to drink some tea. Anne opened her eyes, pushed the cup away, sloshing liquid across the bedding. Her face bright red and contorted, she screamed, "Get away from me, witch." Then she fell back on the bedding, her arms and legs jerking.

Penelope rushed in and grabbed Elizabeth. She yelled, "Leave my daughter alone, you heathen."

Turning to face Penelope, Elizabeth calmly stated, "If she doesn't drink some more tea, she'll die."

Spittle flying, Penelope screamed, "Leave my house, you devil worshipper." She shoved Elizabeth hard.

Elizabeth stumbled. Her shoulders slumped as she walked to the door.

Half an hour later Reverend Smith accompanied by five deacons arrived at Elizabeth's. Entering the house, they grabbed her and took her to the parsonage which had a small room on one side. They pushed her inside.

"Why are you putting me in here, Reverend Smith?"

"You are accused of being a witch."

"But I'm not," she whispered.

Reverend Smith shook his head but remained silent. He kept his lips pressed together as he backed out the door. It shut with a thud and Elizabeth heard the rasp of the bolt.

Falling to her knees, she bowed her head and began praying, "Our Father who art in heaven...."

Reverend Smith, Deacon Jones, and Ruth Green returned in late afternoon. Ruth brought her supper and she set the food down on the small table along one wall; none of the three said anything as they watched Elizabeth eat. After she finished, Deacon Jones took a rope and bound Elizabeth's feet together. He placed a candle on the table in front of her.

"Aren't you going to release me?" Elizabeth said. She looked beseechingly at each person.

Turning his back to her, Reverend Smith commanded Ruth Green, "Don't let her sleep," and then he and Deacon Jones left.

Elizabeth turned to Ruth and said, "You don't believe I'm a witch do you?" Three months ago she had delivered Ruth's daughter.

Shaking her head, Ruth averted her eyes and stared at the floor.

A couple of hours later, Elizabeth's feet throbbed as tears flowed down her cheeks. Weeping silently, she prayed, "Please merciful God, forgive them."

In the middle of the night Elizabeth started to dream about her baby. Her head fell forward. She awoke with a start when Ruth grabbed her shoulder and started shaking it. She stared into Ruth's blood shot eyes. Ruth bit her lip and looked away.

Every time Elizabeth nodded off, someone woke her. The second time Deacon Jones swam into view. A chill coursed through her body as she looked into his eyes.

After forty-eight sleepless hours she began hallucinating. When Deacon Martin awoke her she saw William. She mumbled, "Why are you shaking me, it isn't time to go to church."

Four hours later Reverend Smith entered the room and watched as she slumped forward only to awaken as Martin rudely shook her. In his hands Reverend Smith held a sheet of paper, a quill, and an ink bottle. Striding over to Elizabeth, he bent down and placed his mouth against her ear. He whispered, "Sign this confession and then you can sleep."

Elizabeth's eyelids drooped. She mumbled, "What do you want me to sign, Reverend Smith?"

Elizabeth's eyes closed and her chin fell against her chest.

Reverend Smith grabbed a fistful of hair and jerked her head up. Elizabeth's eyes popped open.

"Sign this, to consecrate your marriage."

Nodding, Elizabeth smiled and said, "I love William, where is he?"

"Here, take the quill and sign, Elizabeth."

Reverend Smith placed the sheet on the table; as he did Elizabeth fell forward, her face covering the document.

Martin pulled her erect and Reverend Smith dipped the quill in the ink and then forced it into Elizabeth's hand.

"Sign here, Elizabeth." Reverend Smith guided her hand.

Elizabeth managed to scrawl her name. When she finished Reverend Smith snatched up the signed confession. Martin eased her face back down unto the table. Reverend Smith nodded and Martin unbound her feet. As they left, the sound of snoring filled the room.

A week later they held her trial in the town meeting hall which they used for resolving secular matters. As Deacon Jones led her into the packed hall, Elizabeth looked around at the faces. Many she had helped. A dull ache engulfed her insides as she noted their serious demeanor. Reverend Smith stood waiting at the front. There were two empty chairs placed six feet apart and Deacon Jones took her to the one on the left.

In a booming voice Reverend Smith called out, "Will William Keane please come forward?"

William rose in the back and worked his way to the center aisle and approached Reverend Smith who motioned him to sit in the right hand chair. William had not seen Elizabeth since they imprisoned her. He looked over at her and smiled and she smiled back.

Reverend Smith began, "Are you William Keane?"

"Yes."

"Are you the husband of the accused, Elizabeth Keane?"

"Yes."

"Your wife is a healer, is she not?"

"Yes."

"Has she ever consorted with heathen Indians?"

William swallowed as he glanced at Elizabeth. "No!" She learned how to brew willow tea from them but she has saved many lives."

"Then she has consorted with those Devil Worshipers?"

"Yes, but…"

Reverend Smith cut William off before he could finish. "You may step down."

"I call on Penelope Wilson to come forward."

Penelope strode down the aisle, took her seat, and glared at Elizabeth. There were dark circles under her blood shot eyes and she twisted a fold of her dress as she waited for Reverend Smith's questions.

"Are you Penelope Wilson?"

"Yes."

"Do you have a nine-year-old daughter named Anne?"

"Yes."

"She is sick, is she not?"

"Yes."

"You asked the accused to help her, did you not?"

"Yes."

"How did the accused treat your daughter?"

"She gave her devil worshiper tea."

"How do you know it was a heathen brew?"

"Because my daughter saw Elizabeth with a heathen Indian. Elizabeth told Anne she learned how to make willow bark tea from them."

"Is the accused a witch?"

Penelope pointed at Elizabeth, and shouted, "Yes! My Anne recognized her when Elizabeth treated her."

After Penelope stepped down Reverend Smith turned to Elizabeth and asked, "Are you a witch?"

Elizabeth shook her head and cried out, "No, I am not!"

"No, I have your signed confession right here."

Reverend Smith held up the paper and displayed it to the crowd.

Handing it to her he said, "Is that not your signature, Elizabeth?"

She stared at the scrawl, the paper rattled.

"Answer me please."

Everyone in the room leaned forward; in back some cupped their ears.

Her dry throat constricted. She managed to whisper, "Yes, it is, but I'm not a witch."

"Read what it says, Elizabeth."

In a soft quavering voice she read, "I confess that I am a witch and devil worshiper."

The sounds of gasps filled the room; some people shook their heads and said no not her.

In the back William's stomach convulsed and he shoved through the crowd. Going outside, he fell to his knees. Vomit spewed out between his fingers.

Inside, Reverend Smith intoned, "You will be hanged this Friday morning. May God forgive you."

The sun shone down from a vivid blue sky; the rope creaked and groaned under its weight. As the body swung back and forth, its shadow darkened a patch of earth.

The court made William pay for the food Elizabeth ate during her incarceration. Anne died three days after they hung her. The congregation buried Anne's body in the cemetery next to the church. The number of new graves increased dramatically during the next year. They buried Elizabeth's remains in an unmarked grave in a cleared field outside of town. In a few years any signs of disturbance there vanished.

Twist of Fate

The roar of its engines had long faded, but Bob, his stomach churning, continued to watch the plane as it became smaller and smaller. He would miss Evan and his companionship, particularly during the deer season when he'd have to hunt alone. When the plane disappeared, he turned to the petite, blond, woman who stood beside him wringing her hands with tears glistening in her eyes.

"He will be alright, Paula, you know he will."

Bob gave Paula a fierce hug as she sobbed against his chest.

"Let's go home."

She nodded, sniffling as she wiped her eyes with the backs of her hands. They drew apart and started back, hand in hand, to the airport parking ramp.

Ten months later found Bob driving to his favorite hunting spot by himself. The road snaked ahead, the white line on the highway's edge difficult to see. Fog rolled across in places and he strained to see. A form, ghost like, rose out of the mist and he braked; his blood running cold, as the animal slipped across the macadam just ahead of his hood. A large rack decorated its head and he shook his head; he'd hunted for four days and had only gotten a fleeting glimpse of a small buck on Saturday. The past Friday he had put his ground blind next to the stand where Evan hunted the last ten years. The stand was no longer there, the tree rotted, its trunk had snapped and carried the platform to the ground where it lay in splintered pieces. A short jagged snag that looked like an extended index finger was all that remained of the once magnificent oak. Three rungs were still attached and he smiled thinking about when he and Evan built it at the end of this ridge that overlooked the river. Evan had shot six deer from it.

Bob saw the turnoff just ahead, his lights illuminated the parking area and he saw it stood empty. Pulling in, he got out and opened the rear door of his Subaru Outback to get his backpack and gun out. The calls of ducks and Tundra swans feeding in the refuge made him think of Evan. A large athletic boy, Evan did well in sports but never did very well in his studies. Bob pursed his lips recalling the time he and Paula attended Evan's tenth grade high school conferences.

Evan's biology teacher, Mrs. Olson, a plump woman with a pleasant face and stray wisps of brown hair falling over her eyes; blew them out of the way and smiled. "I just love Evan, he is such a great kid, but I had to give him the D."

"How can we help?"

"If you could just get him to turn in his work I could at least give him a C."

She searched a stack of papers and took out one to show them. "This is the only paper he turned in."

Handing it to him, she sat back and looked expectantly at both of them. Bob saw the large red A scrawled on its top and shook his head. He handed it to Paula who rolled her eyes.

"We'll see what we can do."

A pickup pulled into the parking area and its tires crunched on the gravel bringing Bob out of his reverie. Its lights blinded him, but not before he saw its Michigan's license plate. He wondered why someone that far away would come to Minnesota to hunt. Two men got out; one a large man with a big head and an average sized guy dressed all in camouflage which surprised Bob.

"Hi, you come way over here to hunt deer? Don't you have big bucks in the UP?"

The two men chuckled. The tall one with the big gut said, "No, not like you have here."

A niggling of irritation surged through Bob. "Where are you going to hunt?"

The camouflaged guy responded. "I'm going to hunt at the base of the hill just beyond where the trail divides. I shot at a massive ten point buck with a deformed rack there on opening day, but missed. I took the shot from the valley floor at about ninety yards."

"I can't tell you where to hunt, but yesterday I set up my blind on that small ridge that extends out from the base of the hill you are talking about."

Camouflaged guy shrugged. "I guess I'll have to change my plans and go up the left hand valley."

As Bob turned away and started out, the two men were getting their equipment out of the back of their truck. His blind stood next to a well used deer trail, and there were two large fresh scrapes within fifty yards of it. Bob glanced overhead and saw Orion the Hunter and Taurus. The stars shown brightly, and when he looked at the eastern horizon only a faint smudge of light shown there. He had plenty of time to get to his setup. As he walked along through the wet leaves carpeting his path, his thoughts turned back to Evan.

When he went off to college, Paula and he hoped that Evan's study habits would change. He attended Winona State and during the fall when they went to visit, Evan took them to the Weaver Bottoms, a refuge for waterfowl fifteen miles north of Winona. The refuge held many Tundra swans and ducks, and they had sat and watched the birds. As he listened to the feeding water fowl, Bob thought of the Tower of Babel.

"How is school going?"

"Okay, we should go deer hunting down here, Dad. South of Winona there is a lot of state land, we could hunt there."

"Don't change the subject."

When they left they both hugged him. Evan had to bend down to hug his mom and Bob laughed and said, "Remember to study hard."

Evan nodded. "I will, I'll also check it out about hunting, too."

When he came home at the end of the school year they sat him down at the kitchen table for a talk. Bob looked at Paula and she nodded. "I sorry, but your mom and I aren't going to help you with college anymore."

Evan scowled. "How am I going to pay?"

"You'll have to figure that out for yourself."

Evan got a job with Tom Sands Construction Company for the summer and made good money.

Tom, Bob's friend, met him for lunch about once a week at Betty's cafe. Bob got to the restaurant first, opened the finger smudged door, and was greeted by the delicious smells of hamburgers and new potato French fries coming from the grill. Taking note of the meatloaf special listed on the blackboard, he walked over to the counter, and slid onto the cracked vinyl stool cover.

Phyllis, a big boned woman with ample boobs and a large bottom who worked as Betty's daytime waitress, came over. "What will it be today, Sugar?"

A man slid onto the stool beside Bob and said in a deep bass voice, "I'll take the special."

Phyllis threw up her hands and winked at Bob. "I was asking your friend here, wise guy."

Bob swiveled around to face Tom. "How is Evan working out?"

Tom clapped Bob on the back with his big calloused hand. "Man, what a worker and he sure learns quick. I am going to hate to see him leave at the end of summer."

Evan transferred from Winona to Mankato and changed his major to elementary education. He also applied for student loans and got them.

That fall he talked Bob into hunting deer on the state land south of Winona.

"I know you love bird hunting, Dad, but let's give deer a try."

On the way out to build their stands, Evan pointed out a number of bare patches of ground and saplings with their bark rubbed off. The bare patches of ground had intersecting lines running through them.

"You say rutting bucks scrape these with their hooves?"

Evan laughed. "Yeah, I read about it, when their testosterone rises this is one of the ways the big boys vent their sexual frustration."

"What about the saplings?"

"The bucks rub those with their antlers to polish them and remove the velvet."

The first year Bob shot a big doe from a stand they built halfway out on the ridge. Evan hunted from the oak stand, he saw some deer, but failed to get a decent shot.

They hunted all four years Evan attended Mankato. Through hard work, he graduated with a 3.4 grade point average in the spring of 1997, but his college loans mounted, and he faced a considerable debt when he finished. Unable to get a permanent job, he came home to Pine City and subbed in the school district, living with Paula and Bob.

A short while after Evan came home, Bob's office phone rang, and Evan's number appeared in the window.

"Hello, Dad?"

"Yeah, this is Dad. What's up?"

"I'm thinking about joining the army reserves to pay for my loans. What do you think?"

"I don't see any major conflicts on the horizon; I think it is a good idea."

Bob stepped on a stick and it broke with a crack, sending a chill racing down his spine. He had reached the small ridge, so he turned off the trail and climbed the twenty feet to its top, wading through a foot of leaves. Looking behind, he saw the Michigan man coming up the trail, his flashlight bobbing and weaving like a firefly flitting over grass in a summer field. As he followed its beam, he saw it veer to the left and go up the left hand valley and disappear. A smile creased his face and he proceeded along the top of the hogback until he reached his blind where he set his backpack down, took out a small black bottle and a cotton wick, which he carried over to a tree whose branches hung over the deer trail. He removed the bottle's cap and the rank smell of doe urine sprang out like an Evil Genie from a rubbed lamp. A convenient branch tip hung low enough so he slipped the saturated wick over its end and returned to the tent. As he stared out the front window, the forest slowly became light enough for him to distinguish individual shapes, so he placed a primer into the basket at the rear of the breech on his black powder gun and settled in.

Evan went to basic at Fort Leonard Wood in Missouri, and after six months of training he returned home.

"They wanted me to go to the Defense Language Institute in Monterrey but I turned them down. They also wanted me to be an officer, I said no again. I did volunteer to help during the compass course, though."

"How long do you have to be in the reserves?"

"Six years."

Glancing at the dangling wick, Bob thought about what happened last year when Evan had a chance to shoot a large buck. Around eleven on the day after opening, Bob heard rustling leaves from something coming fast. Evan appeared, and as he approached Bob, he saw his son's flushed face.

Evan stood below his stand breathing hard. "I missed a big one, Dad."

"What happened?"

Evan waved his arms around and his voice rose. "I saw this buck sneaking up the hill and realized he would pass right by my stand. I waited and he came within thirty-five yards and stood broadside to me sniffing the wick I'd hung out. I put the gun right on him and pulled the trigger, but only the cap went off. The buck bolted and disappeared over the hill."

Bob shook his head. "Didn't you make sure your bullet was seated properly?"

Evan grimaced. "Remember when I shot that doe yesterday? Well, I reloaded and must not have tapped the bullet home."

"How big was his rack?"

Evans eyes enlarged. "A big ten pointer, but one of his tines on the right side extends backwards and looks like a corkscrew."

Bob eased himself up ignoring the pain coming from his knees. "As long as you are here we might as well eat. Too bad you missed him."

Bob thought about what happened last February. Evan's unit, a transportation company based out of Plymouth, Minnesota, had been activated when he had only two more months to serve. They arrived in Kuwait in March and the invasion of Iraq began in April. His unit followed the invasion force closely, supplying fuel for the advancing army.

Leaves rustled on the hillside, and Bob glanced out the side window and saw a huge deer ambling down the trail, its rack raking against trail side branches. Bob's heart raced when it got close enough for him to see the corkscrew tine on the rack's right side. The buck stopped and paused every few feet and tested the air, when he got to the wick he put his muzzle against the dangling cotton pad and sniffed. The buck stood broadside to Bob only twenty-five yards away, he eased off the safety, put the front sight right behind the front shoulder, and pulled the trigger. A cloud of blue smoke obscured Bob's vision, but when it cleared he saw the buck lying on its side under his wick. As he watched, the animal's right hind hoof twitched. He jumped up, knocking his chair over, and reached for the zipper with a shaking hand. Fumbling around while cursing, he finally managed to unzip the opening and get out. As he ran to the buck, he saw its eyes glaze over. He stood shaking, his pulse hammering in his ears. Rummaging in his pack, he took out a cleaning packet and put on rubber gloves. The buck weighed a ton, he struggled gutting it, and by the time he finished his clothes were soaked.

On the way to get the deer cart from his vehicle, he knew he'd have to have help. Evan had always been there before, and together they'd wrestled many deer out of the woods. After he got back to where the buck lay, he left the cart and went in search of the Michigan guy who'd gone up the left hand valley. The guy sat on the hillside half-way up; fortunately, he had changed into blaze orange. Bob introduced himself and Ed did the same. He agreed to assist Bob, and when he saw the buck his eyes widened and he whistled.

Ed grabbed Bob's hand and pumped it. "Holy shit that is one big buck, too bad I missed him."

"Take my picture?"

"Sure."

Bob handed Ed the camera and lifted the buck's head. He smiled when Ed pushed the button.

Bob had to back his Subaru against the road bank because when they tried lifting the deer into the back they couldn't. With the tailgate inches above the ground they were able to slide the carcass in. Bob gave Ed a high-five and then he left to return to hunting.

"Good luck."

"Let me know how much he scored will you?"

"Sure thing."

As Bob opened the car door, his cell phone rang and he reached in and took it from his pocket. When he placed it to his ear he heard sobbing. An icy hand grabbed his heart, and he put his hand against the door jamb to keep from falling. Finally Paula managed to say, "The soldiers are here, Bob, Evan was killed near the Baghdad airport three days ago."

They had Evan's remains cremated. When they picked Evan's urn up from the funeral home Bob removed the cover and slipped in the picture. On its back he'd written, *This one is for you, Evan, you earned him. Love, Dad.*

A Love Square

Leaves rustled to her right, Julia glanced in that direction and spotted a large fox squirrel. It searched the ground and then paused, dug its paws into the dirt, and snatched a nut with its mouth. The squirrel headed for the large shag hickory Julia sat under, and she smiled. When it reached the tree, the squirrel scampered up its truck, its claws clacking on the bark, and it climbed unto the branch just above her. Framed against the blue sky, it sat chewing the nut, rotating it with its paws. Julia took a deep breath, aimed the thirty-two magnum and squeezed the trigger with her gloved hand. The squirrel lifted off the branch, floated down, and landed with a thud ten yards away. When she picked it up she grinned, the squirrel no longer had a head. She slipped it into her pouch, and turned for home. Eight animals, her limit, now weighted her jacket.

When she got home, she cleaned the squirrels and got out her special pan, a large cast iron one that required two hands to handle. The kitchen clock showed her she had plenty of time to fix Kevin's favorite meal.

At five-thirty, right on time, she heard the back door open and then Kevin came into the kitchen. He stopped, sniffed, came up behind her, and placed his arms around her waist.

"You know you could lose some weight."

She butted him and he grunted. "Go sit down at the table, Smartass."

A glob of gravy flew from the pan and plopped down beside the burner so she slowed her stirring. The bastard, she knew she looked good, her weight finally within five pounds of when they married.

After the meal, Kevin stood, patted his stomach, and headed down the hall. When he got to the bedroom doors, he turned left rather than right and sat down in front of the computer. She followed him, and she stared at the flickering screen. Seven months ago she went off the pill without telling him. As she shed weight their love making increased, but for some reason the last month they had only done it twice, the last time a week ago.

"Don't you want to go into the bedroom?"

"No, I have to finish this report."

Julia slumped, turned, and went back out into the kitchen and collapsed into her chair. Tears glistened in her eyes as she thought about how she had met him.

The flock of thirty mallards began their second circle and she placed the duck call to her mouth and gave the feeder. Barney, her yellow lab, shook, pushed his wet coat against her leg, and whined. She shoved back pushing him down and he quivered, his big brown eyes focused on the lead green head which had cupped wings. Her heart sped up as the ducks tilted and plunged toward the decoys. When they were just above the water, they flapped their wings and put their feet down as Julia shouldered her automatic twelve gauge and aimed at the lead bird. She pulled the trigger and it crumpled and cart wheeled sending up a small geyser when it hit. Another two quick shots and two more drakes floated in the decoys. Barney jumped in with a big splash, chose the closest one, and swam with powerful strokes toward it.

After waiting for another hour, she spotted a flock of blue bills coming from the north. They skimmed low over the channel, the strong wind pushing them fast. When they were thirty yards away, she swung on the lead bird and fired. It folded, plunged out of sight, and she zeroed in on the second one. The automatic punched her shoulder as the duck spun and fell, landing with a splat.

After she took care of the ducks, she waded out to pick up her decoys. The cold seeped through her waders, and she shivered as she reached for the last one.

"Hello, who are you?"

Julia looked toward the shore where a tall, slender man stood patting Barney.

"Who are you?"

"I'm Kevin Driscoll. I had to find out who you were."

Julia waded to shore, put down her sack of decoys, and extended her slender hand. "I am Julia Kimball."

A warm, calloused hand grabbed hers. "Glad to meet you. I just had to find out who the great shot is."

"How did you do?"

Kevin's ebony eyes twinkled and a smile creased his tanned face, exposing white uneven teeth. "I didn't get a shot. Someone always got them before I had a chance."

Julia's face became hot. A tendril of her blond hair fell over her blue eyes and she brushed it away, tucking it back under her hat. "Do you come here often?"

"No, but I might if you do. Do you usually hunt alone?"

Tears slid down her cheeks. "I always hunted with my Dad, but he passed away last year."

Kevin's smile disappeared. "I am sorry to hear that. I was just going to ask you to go hunting sometime."

Julia wiped her tears away, and her pupils dilated as she stared into Kevin's eyes. "Thank you for your sympathy. I accept." She smiled. "Maybe I will find out how good a shot you are," and she laughed.

Julia's lips quivered recalling what happened on that first date.

While they waited for ducks to shoot they talked.

"What kind of music do you like?"

"Country Western."

"No kidding, who is your favorite artist?"

"Willy Nelson."

Julia grinned. "I like him too, but my favorite is Randy Travis."

A flock of mallards began circling and as they came in over the decoys Kevin whispered, "I've got the green head on the right, you take the left one."

After Barney retrieved the birds, they resumed their conversation.

"Do you like to dance?"

"Yeah, I do."

"What, waltz, tango, fox trot?"

Julia's eyes widened and she laughed. "How did you know?"

Splashes sounded from the decoys and they turned to see five wood ducks swimming in the spread. Julia looked at Kevin who nodded, she jumped up, and Kevin did the same. The wood ducks' heads swiveled around and they sprang into the air. Five shots rang out and all five plummeted into the pond.

"Goddamn, you are not only good but fast."

Julia giggled. "Aw shucks, Mister, you can just call me Annie."

Kevin cocked an eyebrow. "I suppose you are also an electrical engineer."

She laughed out loud. "No, but I have a chemical engineering degree from Minnesota."

Drawing in a deep breath, she sighed and thought about the first years of their marriage.

Ann, a chubby strawberry blond asked, "Aren't you going to play your card?"

Roberta, Julia's best friend said, "You were thinking about Kevin weren't you."

Julia nodded, slapped down her card, and took the trick. "I can't believe how good he is. It is like we met through E-harmony."

Ann asked, "He is great in bed, right?"

Julia's face became hot and she laughed, but shivered inwardly. "You got it right, gal, he is one hot dude."

An image of Kevin and her in bed two weeks before this particular monthly card party brought fresh tears.

Julia sat in bed with the blankets tucked around her and talked about how she wanted to have a child.

Kevin jerked the covers off her and reared up. "For Christ's sake will you quit nagging?"

Cool air rushed up her nightgown, goose bumps erupted on her arms, and she shivered.

"*Please?*"

Kevin drew back his fist, and shot it forward. It whistled by her ear and punched a hole in the wall right above her head.

Julia's eyes' widened, she placed her hands over them, and burst into tears. Kevin grabbed her arms and forced them down. "*Look at me.*"

She looked at his flushed face and watched his lips curl back and mouth open. "*Don't ever mention having kids again, you hear me?*"

Her stomach churned, but she managed to nod.

The yard light came on and Julia glanced out the window as she thought about Kevin's fortieth birthday party.

After getting out of bed that morning, she stumbled into the bathroom. Kevin had already left for work so she could go ahead with her plans. She flicked on the light switch, went over to the vanity, looked in the mirror, and grimaced. Her once shining hair now lay in dull tangled bunches, there were dark circles under her eyes, and a red rash encircled them. Her waistline

bulged and her thighs strained against her cotton pajamas. She touched her cheek and a moan escaped her lips. When she had asked Kevin for a divorce he slapped her, she had seen stars, and almost blacked out.

"*Don't talk to me about a divorce, I won't give you one.*"

Her ears ringing, she stared at his eyes that looked like black stones as he nodded. Icy fingers grabbed her heart and worked their way down to her stomach.

"*That's right, the slap is only a love tap compared to what I'll do if you try.*"

The only thing they emotionally still connected on was discussing his job. She thought about their talk yesterday they had before she asked for a divorce.

"*I interviewed a guy for the new position in our department today. Do you remember me telling you about Brian Christopher?*"

"*No.*"

"*Well, he worked for us as an intern last summer, his grades aren't the greatest, but he performed really well on the job. I want to hire him but Paul doesn't. What do you think I should do?*"

Julia didn't think much of Paul the head plant manager. A big man, he used intimidation to bully employees who didn't stand up to him.

She smirked, "Hire him."

"Okay."

"What did Rita think?" Rita, Kevin's secretary, was bright, but lazy and Julia disliked her.

Kevin chortled. "Her tongue hung out and her eyes feasted on him all the time she saw him."

Her reflection reappeared; she resolved to go on a diet and go off the pill. Maybe she could have a child to love if she couldn't escape Kevin.

Later that day she hummed as she set the table. The savory smell of squirrel wafted from the kitchen and she set two goblets on the tablecloth along with a bottle of Carmenere. Earlier she had wrapped Kevin's gift, a thirty-two magnum pistol that she knew he wanted for deer hunting. The phone rang and she set the wrapped package down.

"Hello, Julia?"

"Kevin?"

"I'm sorry, Hon, I have to work late. You didn't make anything special for my birthday did you?"

"No." The knuckles of her hand whitened as she wished her fingers were around his neck.

"Don't wait up."

She grabbed the skillet from the stove, tromped out to the garage, yanked the garbage can lid off, and dumped the gravy out. Some of the liquid ran down the side but she didn't give a damn. When she got back to the table she uncorked the wine and filled a glass to the brim. In no time the bottle stood empty and she staggered off to bed.

Her eyes fluttered open and she heard steady breathing. Kevin lay next to her on his back, his chest rising and falling. She looked at the clock and saw 3:35. Her head hurt, and her dry mouth tasted terrible. As she took a deep breath, she detected a faint odor. She lay there trying to place it, but after a few minutes she rolled over and went back to sleep.

Julia picked up the Redbook that lay on the table. A dark haired woman in

a party dress with a smile plastered on her face looked back. Julia began think-
ing about what happened at this year's Power Plant Christmas party.

Happy party noises greeted Kevin and Julia when they arrived. As they
entered the recreation room, a tall dark haired woman sauntered over on stiletto
heels. The top of her dress rode just above the aureoles of her breasts and Julia
marveled at their size and the ability of the red satin to contain them.

Rita winked. "Hi guys; go over and get yourselves a drink."

Kevin's face reddened. "Yeah, we will have to do that."

As they brushed by her, Julia caught a whiff of Rita's perfume, and she
gasped.

Kevin stopped and looked at her. "Anything wrong?"

Julia just shook her head, afraid if she said anything it would be bad. They
wandered over to the bar. A young buffed guy with diamond studs in his ears
and black curly hair falling over his collar stood in front of it. Kevin asked,
"How is it going, Brian?"

"Great, I'll have to show you my new F150 later."

"Ah, Julia, I'd like you to meet Brian Christopher, he is my newest hire."

Julia smiled and extended her hand. Brian clasped it and gave it a little
squeeze, but by the look he gave her she knew he had no interest in talking to
her.

Julia set the magazine down.

Three days before Christmas Kevin worked late; when he called he said
they were working out details on a plan to cut greenhouse gas emissions. After
Julia talked with him she waited for a couple of hours and then drove to Rita's
house, whose address she'd looked up and programmed into her GPS. When she
got there, she saw Kevin's Ford Explorer sitting in the driveway. She parked just
beyond it and pounded the steering wheel as tears ran down her face. After a few
minutes she composed herself and drove home.

Four days after Christmas Kevin called again and said he'd be late; they were
still working on the greenhouse gas plan. After Julia put the phone down, she went
to the kitchen, found a pair of rubber gloves, slipped them on, and then went to the
gun safe in the den from which she removed the thirty-two magnum. Going out in

the living room, she turned on the television and watched it for an hour.

When she arrived at Rita's, a Ford pickup sat in the driveway, and she frowned. She parked across the street and decided to wait. After twenty minutes a man came out of the house and when he passed by the driveway light she got a glimpse of his face and she laughed. Her fingers drummed out a Willy Nelson tune as she watched the tail lights of the truck disappear down the street.

Julia rose, walked down the hall past the spare bedroom, and glanced in. Kevin sat before the computer typing away; she sighed and went into the master bedroom.

After Kevin left for work the next day, Julia typed out a note using Word. When she finished, she slipped it into a blank envelope. She went into the kitchen, grabbed the phone, and punched in Roberta's number.

"Hello, Roberta?"

"Julia?"

"Yeah."

"What's up?"

Julia took a deep breath, told her heart to slow down and said, "Would you do me a favor?"

"Sure, what is it?"

"I am having trouble with my car and forgot to tell Kevin what to pick up at the grocery store. It is a long list so I just can't call him. Would you mind dropping if off at the plant?"

"No problem, I'll swing by in about an hour and get it."

Fifty minutes later the doorbell rang and Julia went to the door with the note. She handed the envelope to Roberta. "Hi, I really appreciate this."

"Hey no problem, who do I give this to?"

"Give it to the receptionist." Julia frowned. "Oh, I just thought, I forgot to sign it. Put Kevin's name on it."

As she waited, Julia couldn't sit still. She tried reading, but kept glancing at the clock. At four-thirty the phone rang, she jumped up, sprinted to the kitchen, and snatched it up.

"Hello Julia?"

"Yes."

"I'm really sorry, Hon, but I'm going to have to work late."

As she put the phone back in the charger a shiver crawled down her spine, she hoped her plan worked.

At around seven she parked across the street from Rita's, glanced at the driveway, and smiled when she saw Kevin's SUV. She slipped plastic bags over her athletic shoes, grabbed the thirty-two magnum with her gloved hands, and fast walked over to Rita's entrance door. She pushed against it and it opened a crack allowing her to slip into the darkened hall.

"I don't believe you, you Goddamn slut."

"Brian is just a friend, you have to believe me."

Their voices came from the room at the end of the hall. Julia heard a slap and then Rita sobbing as she rushed down the hall with the magnum held in front of her. She charged into the kitchen and saw Rita crying in front of the sink with Kevin holding and shaking her. Rita's head snapped back and forth, her eyes rounded and she screamed when she saw Julia. Kevin let her go and started to turn as Julia shoved the gun against his temple and fired. Blood, bone chips, and bits of brain splattered on the cabinet door next to the sink. Julia swung the gun and fired a bullet into Rita's chest. As the bodies toppled to the floor she dropped the magnum and ran.

The police arrived at 9:30 AM the next day and told her about Kevin and Rita. When Rita's car pooling friend arrived to pick Rita up, she had gone into the house and discovered the bodies. The lead detective, a man with a crooked nose and pale blue eyes, told her the police suspected it was a murder-suicide, but the investigation had just started.

"I know now is not the proper time to talk about your relationship with Kevin, but we will want to interview you in the near future."

Julia sat wringing her hands and as she wiped tears away she sniffled and said, "I can understand that Detective Burns."

"Will next Tuesday be alright?"

Julia nodded,"Yes, that will be fine." .

Four weeks later she found a small article on the case buried on a back page. The investigation had not turned up anything new and was still ongoing. After she finished reading it, she picked up the kit, and walked into the bathroom. Her period was late and she just wanted to make sure.

"Ambush"

They walked along the side of the gravel road, but when they saw him they jumped back into the ditch. As he approached, they started to run. Drawing abreast of the group caused them to move jerkily and they changed directions repeatedly, not knowing which way to turn. A female stuck her head under the lower strand of barbed wire, but then withdrew it. Their eyes bulged as they attempted to escape. As he drove by, they stopped and watched until he disappeared. A mile out of Buffalo, Wyoming, these were the first antelope he saw this morning. Proceeding up the wide valley, he saw antelope feeding in the hay fields and others mixed with cattle in the pastures. Some nice bucks, their antlers curving in to form a heart. On the Boone and Crockett web site, he learned that bucks with horns that did this, were a trophy.

Stan, a forty year old pilot for Mesabi airline, lived with his wife Susan in St. Paul, Minnesota. Married for ten years, they didn't have any children and both had decided they didn't want any. A natural athlete, he competed in triathlons in the summer and played amateur hockey in the winter. He also enjoyed both downhill and cross-country skiing; however, his first love was hunting. Born in a small town in west-central Minnesota he grew up hunting duck, pheasant, and deer. Many deer fell to his gun; two years ago he had bagged a ten point buck that scored high in Boone and Crockett.

His brother told him, "You ought to hunt antelope. I shot my pronghorn last year at two hundred and eighty yards. I drilled him through the heart."

He'd fallen in love with muzzle loading five years ago and shot his trophy buck at seventy-one yards with his black powder gun. To make his hunt more challenging, he planned to shoot his antelope with it.

Twenty-five miles out of Buffalo, he pulled over and stopped. On his east side were two adjacent sections of state land, there were no signs, but he identified them from the map. They lay across from a small reservoir where the road jogged at the end of the lake. He drove a mile north and parked. To the northeast he saw a ranch off a road that intersected the one he was on. The buildings were the only ones for miles. On the side-hill behind the house a small herd of whitish animals grazed, lit by the morning sun. Training his binoculars on them, he saw they were antelope, one had horns. It was difficult to get on private property; most ranchers charged a hunting fee. It surprised him that most requested payment for even crossing their land to access public areas.

Across from him, a wide draw curved away to the southeast. Stan got out of his vehicle and decided to walk up it, following a cattle trail. The path lead to a wide meadow dotted with patches of sage brush. Rock outcroppings crowned the ridge tops; the gray and orange, lichen covered rocks formed interesting patterns and shapes. Some reminded Stan of medieval fortresses; their crenelated tops sticking above the ridge line. In the dust of the path, there were many hoof prints, and he wondered if they were antelope or deer.

He stopped and put a primer on the nipple of his gun to be ready to shoot. Glassing the area ahead, he didn't see any antelope. A small animal darted out from under his feet, his heart lurched, and he shouldered his rifle. As the cottontail disappeared into the brush he smiled.

A cool morning, he wore a fleece shirt under his camouflage jacket. As he climbed and then crossed the meadow, he perspired. The October sun beat down from an azure sky, so he stopped, took off the fleece, and put it in his backpack. His clammy tee-shirt stuck to his skin. When he raised his arms to remove the shirt, he grimaced; he would have to stay downwind from any antelope if he wanted to get close. His camouflage would help; maybe he'd take off his blaze orange cap when he made a stalk.

To the west the snow covered peaks of the Big Horns stood out against the sharp horizon. No wind rustled the grass which didn't happen very often on this Wyoming plain.

As he approached the backside of the ridge, he saw a steep draw that went down to a wide basin. He assumed if antelope were going to go over this hump they'd come up through the draw.

A lone willow tree grew about one third of the way across the basin and he wondered why it happened to be there. He'd walked a couple of miles, but knew this was still state land. From his map, the bottom of the ridge formed the boundary with the rancher's acreage.

Walking over to the slope, he scanned the terrain for a hiding place. On this side of the draw, a fourth of the way down, he spotted a large rock. Tall clumps of sage brush grew on its downhill side. Ambling over to the boulder, he sat down behind it. This would be an excellent spot to post. After sitting, he removed his cap and replaced it with a camouflaged boonie he'd carried in his pocket.

While waiting, he studied the basin. As the sun rose higher in the sky, shadows ebbed and flowed across the opposite ridges creating random patterns. The countryside reminded him of a giant's rumpled blanket. The pungent smell of sage filled his nostrils, a pleasant odor, but so strong it burned in his nose.

Directly overhead, a hunting red tail hawk wheeled and soared, calling out with screeches. Its vivid tail twisted as it maneuvered in flight. He watched as it swooped down and landed in the top of the willow tree. Raising his binoculars, he scanned the basin. A long way away three antelope stood out against the yellowish grass. The two on the far side were bucks and he watched as they charged each other, locked horns, and twisted their heads, lowering them to the ground. They backed apart and one turned and ran: the victor chased it for a short distance. Moving his binoculars to the right, he spotted a hunter advancing up the middle of the basin. He had on a blaze orange hat and coat which made him standout against the subdued yellows and browns of the prairie.

Hearing an engine, he swung his glasses to the left and saw the rancher on a four- wheeler headed toward the hunter. Stan caught movement out of his left eye. Looking in that direction, he spotted three antelope doe approaching from the north along the base of the ridge. He reached for his gun and raised it to his shoulder. Two continued running along the base, but one turned up toward him. Six more does appeared, following the one headed for him. His heart accelerated, a buck would probably be chasing after the females.

The does thundered by, passing the rock only twenty yards away from him. Detecting movement at the base of the draw, he turned his head to get a better look. A buck with a good set of horns started up the draw. Stan's heart hammered in his chest. A shot came from down in the basin, but he continued following the buck. It ran up the gully, but then slowed to a walk as it neared his hiding place. When the buck's chest became visible, Stan placed the front sight on its shoulder and pulled the trigger. The gun boomed as the bullet slammed into its flank; the buck toppled over onto its side.

Jumping up, he walked to the animal. Its hind legs gave a feeble kick as its eyes glazed over.

The four-wheeler starting caused him to look across the basin. Stan watched as the hunter raced away. Putting his binoculars up to his eyes, he saw the rancher sprawled on the ground. His eyes bulged when he realized what must have happened.

Looking back at the antelope, he saw it had died. A shadow passed over him and he looked up to see a soaring turkey vulture.

Slinging his gun over his shoulder, Stan started back; he had to alert the authorities. He broke into a run, but the terrain soon forced him back to a walk. It took him forty-five minutes to hike out and one time he thought he heard the four-wheeler. The wind had come up making it difficult to hear so he wasn't sure. Coming around the last bend, Stan saw his station wagon a short distance away.

Something punched him hard on his shoulder and he fell backward. As he did, he heard the report of a gun. His head slammed into a stone and everything went black.

Stan opened his eyes, his shoulder hurt like hell and blood covered the front of his jacket. A crunching noise approached and he decided to play dead. A gun barrel came into view and a man loomed over him. Adrenaline surged through his body, he reached up, grabbed the barrel, and jerked it to the side. The bastard pulled the trigger, and a small divot appeared right behind his head. Stan wrestled the guy for the weapon. Pulling hard, he forced his assailant to his knees and by twisting and pulling at the same time he wrenched it from the others grasp.

He yelled out, "You son of a bitch."

Stan stood and pointed the gun at the guy's gut while backing away from him. The man snarled something unintelligible and charged. Stan swung the butt at his head; he landed a glancing blow which made a sickening sound when it struck. The man crumpled face- down and lay still.

Gasping for breath, his shoulder hurting like hell, Stan staggered to his feet and headed for his car. The nylon rope he always carried would do for tying this bastard up.

A few yards from his wagon, Stan became nauseated. Liquid surged up out of his stomach, and he leaned over as a stream of vomit splattered to the ground. Wiping his mouth with his hand, he tasted the foul remnants of bile on his tongue. Stumbling forward, he managed to get to his wagon and leaned up against its cool surface as sweat beads popped out on his forehead. Blackness danced at the periphery of his vision, and his head felt light. Slapping himself in the face cleared his head, and he looked for the rope. He found it lying behind the back seat; he grabbed it and staggered back toward the prone man.

He had shouldered the man's rifle and as he drew near, he held it out in front. The man lay in the same position, so Stan set the gun down. As he did, arms reached around from behind, grabbed the weapon, and jerked. Stan almost lost his grip, but managed to hold on as he yanked back.

Stan whirled around and raising his knee, drove it into the man's groin. Screaming, the man fell to his knees and let go. He gagged, leaned forward, and retched. Swiping a sleeve across his mouth, the man looked at Stan and rasped out in a whisper, "You're lucky I didn't shoot you in the head, fucker."

"Get up, you bastard."

Struggling, the man got to his feet; Stan held the 270 semiautomatic on him.

"Start walking."

"Where are we going?"

"See that ranch? You and I are going over there to call the authorities."

Stan walked twenty yards behind. The ranch house seemed miles away, and midway there, the guy turned and rushed him, but Stan shot right in front of his feet and he backed off. By the time they got to the front gate the gun wobbled in Stan's hands and sweat covered his face. Coming into the front yard he said, "You stand over there. Don't try anything or I'll shoot you."

Stan rang the doorbell. His head throbbed, and sweat ran down his neck and mingled with the blood pulsing from his shoulder. He fought to remain conscious.

A curly haired woman with big eyes and large dangling earrings came to the door.

"Yes"

"My name is Stan Gunderson. That man over there shot me. Can you call the sheriff? "

The woman's face reddened and she stammered out, "Oh my God."

Turning around, she disappeared back into the house.

Stan shouted through the screen door, "Hurry up, please; I don't know how much longer I can last."

After a short time, he sensed something in a window to his left; he turned and looked at the glass.

A shot rang out and a hole appeared in the middle of his forehead. Bone and brain matter sprayed out the back of his head as his dead body toppled off the stoop and bounced on the ground.

Coming outside, the woman approached the stocky, dark man with the jagged scar on his right cheek. Smiling when she reached him, she put her arms around his neck and kissed him hard on the lips.

"Nice shot. Your old man's body is lying out in the middle of the basin."

"Are you sure he is dead?"

"Ya, I'm sure. I plugged him just like you did this guy."

"I love you Frank, let's get out of here."

"Have you got all your old man's money?"

"You know I do. It is in a bank in the Bahamas."

The turkey vulture landed and studied the figure on the ground. Satisfied, the bird hopped up on its head and plunged its beak into an eyeball. The massive horns formed a perfect heart, encircling the vulture. A trophy, it would easily qualify for the Boone and Crockett record book.

Two days later the Buffalo's paper screamed out the news in bold print. The manhunt had succeeded. Frank Paulson and Rita Dominic were in custody. Unbeknownst to them, another hunter observed what happened and reached the ranch house shortly after Frank and Rita left. The couple was alleged to have shot an antelope hunter, Stan Gunderson, from St. Paul, Minnesota and alleged to have killed John Dominic, Rita's husband. Gunderson's body, shot twice, once in the shoulder and once in the head, had been found by the front door of the ranch house. The body of John Dominic had been recovered a mile and one-half south of the ranch. Dominic had been shot in the temple.

Artificial

As Scott and his charges entered the ripping room, a high pitched whine assailed his ears and a strong odor of fresh cut lumber filled his nostrils. He liked the smell, but his charges needed noise protection. Reaching in a bin by the door, he took out packets of ear plugs and handed them out. Scott said, "Wait here."

He walked over to Bill and shouted, "Can we talk with Frank?"

Ornery Bill, the foreman, sometimes refused, and made him wait until the shift ended. This was the last stop on the new employee orientation tour. The recent hires had followed Scout like guppies for over two hours, asking inane questions, and he wanted to finish up now. Scott worked for the Balderson Window Company of Elgin, Minnesota. Bill's orders were all new people must meet Frank Vincent.

Bill scowled, hesitated for a minute, but then yelled, "Hey, Frank, these guys want to meet you."

The man in the far corner shut his saw off and came over.

Scott introduced Frank. All the new employees stared at him; a few averted their eyes and looked past him. Some shuffled their feet. Frank winked at Scott and started talking. After Frank finished, he asked if there were any questions. As Frank answered the queries, Scott thought about what happened twenty-nine years ago when Baldersons had expanded. They did a lot of construction and to save money, Baldersons pulled people off the line to help.

Scott shivered and slapped his shoulders with his gloved hands. Frank and he were assembling scaffolding on the outside of the skeletal structure which would become building three. Scott waited on the first tier for Frank to bring more planks so they could go a level higher. He saw Frank coming across the torn up ground with a large one. Because of its size, it partially blocked Frank's view and when he got by the utilities access hole, he stubbed his right foot on a short two by four sticking out of the frozen ground and plunged head first into it. He cried out "Holy shit," as he disappeared.

Scott tore down off the scaffolding and ran over. Dropping down unto his knees, he peered over the edge and saw Frank on his one hand and knees on top of the plank. He held the other hand against his head, blood oozed out between his fingers.

Scott shouted, "How bad are you hurt?"

"I'm bleeding, but I don't think I broke anything."

Scott lay down and extended his arm. "Take my hand."

Frank stood up, but wobbled on his feet, taking a step backward. Scott grabbed for his wrist, caught it, and pulled. Frank struggled and stumbled up the side keeping his one hand tight to his head.

Tom, Jim, and Dave came over. Dave, a supervisor, asked, "What happened?"

Blood covered the top of Frank's jacket collar. He removed his hand.

The men gaped at him wide-eyed. Tom turned white, his irises disappeared, and he fell, bouncing as he landed. Jim yelled, "Jesus, your ear is gone!"

Dave shouted, "Scott call 911 from building two and have them send an ambulance, grab a blanket too. Jim, you help Frank lay down."

Scott sprinted over to the next building, went inside, and punched the 911 button on the phone hanging next to the entry door.

Siren wailing, the ambulance arrived in eight minutes. The paramedics jumped out and ran over. They checked Frank, put him on a stretcher, loaded him into the ambulance, and sped off.

Dave asked, "Tom, are you alright?"

Tom nodded.

"Well then you and Jim get back to work. Scott come with me."

When Dave and Scott arrived at the emergency area of the hospital, they parked in the south lot and ran over to the entrance. They burst through the door and spotted a gray-haired woman sitting behind a desk on the far side of the room. Hurrying over to her, Dave said, "I'm Dave Johnson and this is Scott Crandall. We are from Baldersons and want to see Frank Vincent. They just brought him in."

She nodded. "Yes, he's in ER. Go through those double doors."

They found Frank in the third bed; a white-coated tall thin doctor and a short fat nurse working on him. As they came in, the doctor asked, "Are you from Baldersons?"

Dave answered "Yes."

"Did one of you see this happen?"

Dave looked at Scott who responded, "I did."

"Do you have his ear?"

Scott's forehead wrinkled. "No, why do you want it?"

"We may be able to sew it back on. Can you try and find it?"

"Sure."

Frank mumbled, "Good luck."

He attempted to smile, but it turned into a grimace.

Standing on edge of the hole, Dave commanded, "I'll look for it, you stay here."

Dave climbed down, got on his knees, and crawled around with his head inches from the dirt.

"I see what must have cut his ear off. There is a sharp metal piece on the side of the plank."

"Do you see it?"

"No, I'm going to sift through the dirt with my fingers."

Scott watched as Dave worked up the sides.

Dave stopped, dug in the soil, and yelled, "I think I found it."

He held the object high above his head, looked up, and grinned. After emerging, he showed it to Scott and then wiped off the dark soil on his pant leg.

"Let's go, I hope they can sew this back on."

"God, I hope they can too."

The attempt failed. After a week, Frank came back to work, the side of his head covered with gauze. A month later he came without any bandage.

Scott said, "That is quite a wound. You're lucky you didn't lose any hearing."

"Ya, I guess. My ability to pick up women has suffered."

"You haven't scored since you lost it?"

"Ya, once. I met this woman at Fred's; she thought it cool."

"Can't they make an artificial one?"

"They told me at Mayo they would, but it has to heal first."

His coworkers got used to Frank's lop-sidedness, but new employees gaped. He'd guffaw and then tell them how it happened. After four months he went for his fitting and three weeks later came to work wearing his new ear.

Scott said, "It looks great. How do you keep it on?"

Frank pirouetted. "With a soft adhesive, I take it off at night and put it back on in the morning."

Frank did a lot of carousing and drinking. Everyone knew if he had a hangover; on those days he slept in and didn't take time to glue his ear on. Once and awhile Scott came along with Frank.

A blue cloud of smoke hung just above them. The beat of the loud music reverberated in Scott's head and raucous laughter came from the other end of the bar; a typical night at Fred's. Frank and he perched on their stools downing glass after glass of Bud drafts. Frank wore his Viking cap.

Frank asked, "Who do you think is going to win Sunday's game?"

"The Vikings will."

A large guy wearing a dirty Green Bay jacket and cap sat down on the stool next to Frank.

The burr-headed bar tender with the bicep barbed-wire tattoo said, "What'll it be?"

"Give me a bud draft"

"Coming right up."

The bar tender slid the full glass across the bar into the waiting mitt of the man; he deftly caught it, raised it to his mouth and downed its contents in one long gulp. He slammed it down and swiveled around to face Frank. "The Vikings couldn't beat their own mothers."

Even from the other side of Frank, Scott smelled the guy's rotten breath. His brown teeth looked like a crooked unpainted picket fence with random slats missing and his flattened nose bent to the left.

Frank smirked, "Is that right."

"That's right dickhead, besides, the Vikings play dirty."

Frank glared, "You know what cheese-head? The Pack sucks."

The man came off his stool fast; it toppled and crashed to the floor. Leaping with arms outstretched, he grabbed Frank's head in a half Nelson. He dragged Frank off his cushion, and made a fist with his free hand. Frank twisted and squirmed, trying to get away. Scott saw something fall to the floor, so he reached down and snatched it.

The guy smashed his ham sized fist into Frank's eye.

Scott dangled the object in front of the dick head's red mug and shouted, "You crazy bastard, you just ripped off his ear!"

"Huh?"

Scott yelled, "You dumb-fuck, look at his head."

The guy's eyes popped open wide as he whined, "I didn't mean to.

Shouldn't we call 911 or something?"

Frank and Scott laughed. Scott said, "Don't worry, his ear is counterfeit."

They closed down the bar; drinking round after round, most bought by Ed the packer-backer. The next day Frank's swollen eye sported a purplish ring.

From then on Frank and Scott decided to have some fun. They approached Dave, the supervisor, and told him want they planned. Dave, as crazy as they were said, "Go ahead, just don't come to me if it's reported and you two get into trouble."

Two months later they had there first chance.

Scott, the ripping room team leader, admonished Doug, the new hire, "Remember; be careful around your saw. One careless move and you can kiss a finger or some other body part goodbye. Frank Vincent, who operates the third saw, has never had an accident. You're using the saw next to his, watch and see how he does things."

A couple of hours after lunch, Frank leaned inward, his head inches away from his whirring blade. A second later, an object flew into the air and landed on Doug's saw table. Frank grabbed the side of his head and howled, "Jesus H. Christ." Doug looked over and saw blood flowing out from between Frank's fingers. Frank quavered, "Help"

Doug's face drained of color. He snatched up the object, waved it back and forth, and ran over to Scott.

"Call 911!"

"No."

"What?"

"Frank has to finish his shift first."

"Are you crazy?"

Scott grinned. "Don't worry it is plastic."

"What?"

"Frank's ear is artificial. He lost his real one last year."

Doug looked at Frank who was doubled over.

He snarled, "You shit-heads, I should quit.", but then he turned, laughed, and walked back to his saw.

Through the years they pulled the prank six times and pulled it on ornery Bill when he started. After the joke, he threatened to tell management but, Dave told him, "Go ahead." Fortunately, he didn't, but when the company promoted him, Bill put a stop to all shenanigans. After six months he put the Frank Vincent safety law into effect and told Scott, "Make sure all new hires talk to Frank."

When Frank offered his fake ear to the nearest person, Scott came out of his reverie. The guy hesitated, but then took it. Frank admonished them, "Remember safety first; you don't want to saw your ear off like I did."

Gary, a big man with a lop-sided grin asked, "Did you really cut your ear off with one of these saws?"

Frank chuckled. "You'll have to ask Scott about that after a couple of beers at Fred's."

Charade

The hearse pulled into the cemetery and proceeded to an area where many of the graves had flag standards. A late October day, a raw wind blew as rain slanted down from a gray sky. Many maples stood in this section; the gusts whipped the few remaining leafs off their branches, scattering them on their neighbors.

As the hearse approached, the six old men came to attention. Dressed in parts of uniforms; most wore caps and some military jackets. They leaned into the strong wind, seeming on the verge of toppling over. The oldest, a white-haired man, raised a shaking hand to his forehead. With the Great War over for sixty-four years, their presence constituted a final tribute to a fallen comrade, one of the members of their last bottle club.

The entourage came to a stop. In the lead car, Kathleen opened the door. She clutched two identical red roses in her right hand. After the graveside ceremony a bugler played "Taps." As the last note faded, Kathleen rose from her chair and hobbled to the casket. The smell of newly turned earth filled her nostrils, an odor which she always associated with springtime, not death. Images of bygone days swirled in her head, particularly those of Brockville. Recalling this small Minnesota town along the Mississippi river, she smiled. She remembered when people of Germanic descent attended the protestant church, and the era when it still held services in German.

Ludwig Metzger, Kathleen's future father-in-law and a deacon at Zion's Evangelical church, enjoyed hearing the sermon delivered in his grandfather's native tongue. A big man with a hearty laugh, he had meet Martha through church. A diminutive woman with a serious demeanor, she enjoyed listening to Ludwig talk. He made her smile. They married in the spring of 1894. Martha gave birth to Paul and Robert, identical twins, in May of 1896. When the two boys were two weeks old, the Metzger's had them baptized.

As they grew up, telling them apart proved difficult even for their mother.

"Will you please fill the wood box for me, Paul?"

Robert grinned, "I'll go get him, Ma, he's playing out back."

Telling them apart also perplexed their teachers, but in the fourth grade an incident occurred that allowed everyone to easily distinguish them. At the beginning of the school year, David Keane, a small sickly boy, joined their class. His folks had a small dirt farm where they raised goats and David brought goat's milk to school to have with his lunch. While he was eating one day, Max Richardson approached him. Max, who had been held back two grades, was a large boy with a mean streak. He liked picking on smaller kids, particularly those who were different. Taunting David, he shouted, "Momma's boy, why don't you drink real milk?"

Max grabbed the jar of milk out of David's hand and threw it. When it hit the sidewalk it exploded, sending glass shards and milk in all directions. David's lip quivered and he began crying. Paul and Robert, who were nearby, rushed up and Paul grabbed Max, spinning him around.

"What the hell?" Max yelled, and punched Paul in the eye.

The two grappled and losing their balance went down. Max ended up on top of Paul and started hitting him in the face. Robert tackled Max, attempting to pull him off, but Max maintained his position. Gretchen Bissen screamed and ran in to get Miss Johnson. The principal ended up kicking Max out of school. Paul's eye swelled up and turned an ugly purple color. Until it healed, no one had any problems telling them apart.

After they graduated from eighth grade, they went to work for Schaller brewery. Ludwig, the brew master told Otto Schaller, "My twins will make excellent workers. They're strong and follow orders well."

Already muscular and big like their dad, they were hired. Paul worked on the loading dock and Robert helped on the kettle crew. Both jobs were physically demanding, but the boys did well.

In 1914, when the First World War broke out, the Boche, portrayed as rapists and pillagers, swept through Belgium in their August offensive. In spite of this, Brockville's citizens supported the Germans more than the allied forces. When a U-boat sank the Lusitanian on May 7th 1915; Brockville's sympathies, as well as most of America's, shifted. However, unlike some areas of America, the Germans escaped vilification in Brockville.

The twins became interested in girls when they turned sixteen. Many local dances and barn raisings provided them with ample opportunities to meet women. Blond, blue eyed and natural athletes with rugged good looks, Robert and Paul learned to dance from their mother. Many evenings were spent in the Metzger home with Ludwig playing the piano and the boys dancing with their mother. Ludwig always laughed because Martha only came up to the boys' chests. They enjoyed learning and soon were accomplished hoofers. They had no problem attracting partners. The twins were considered two of the most eligible bachelors in town and many girls pursued them. However, they relished playing the field and neither twin had a serious relationship until Kathleen O'Connell.

The brewery expanded in the fall of 1916. Shamus O'Connell, Kathleen's uncle, told his brother about it.

"Michael, you ought to move to Brockville. Schaller's needs men and what better job is there for an Irishman than brewing beer?"

Michael, along with his family, came to Brockville that autumn. Dennis, the oldest sibling in the family, started working in the brewery when his dad did. In spite of being small, he accepted a job on the loading dock. Like his dad's Morgan horses, he proved to be much stronger than he looked. Assigned the same shift as Paul, Dennis impressed him with his strength and work ethic. The two soon became fast friends. Not quite handsome because of his large nose, Dennis still proved irresistible to the girls. Using his gift of gab and beautiful tenor voice to impress the young ladies of Brockville, he hoped to bed as many of them as possible. Unfortunately, his luck ran out when he got Gretchen Bissen pregnant.

Dennis told Robert and Paul, "Dang if I'm not going to have to marry Gretchen, she is a comely lass but her family dislikes me. Paul, would you be my best man?"

Kathleen, Michael's oldest daughter, a beautiful girl with jet-black hair, a creamy complexion, generous mouth, lively blue eyes, and an ample figure was always smiling and laughing. She also loved to dance. Light on her feet, she appeared to float around the dance floor. Now nineteen, she had started dating at seventeen, but until meeting Paul Metzger she never had more than two or three dates with the same fellow.

Gretchen asked Kathleen, "Will you be my maid of honor? None of my Protestant friends will stand up for me since we're going to be married in your church."

"Yes, I'll be happy to."

At the wedding dance, Paul and Kathleen stared into each other's eyes as they whirled around the dance floor. When Kathleen's neck and cheeks reddened, Paul smiled. As the evening progressed his face also became hot. When holding her close, he felt the soft curves of her body pressing against his. A delicious lavender smell emanated from her and she felt light as a feather.

Grinning widely, Paul said, "You dance divinely, Miss O'Connell."

Smiling back Kathleen replied, "You're not so bad yourself, Mr. Metzger."

For the next two months Paul dated no other girl. Through a Catholic friend of hers, Martha learned about Paul and Kathleen. At the dinner table one night, she asked him about her.

"Have you been seeing Kathleen O'Connell?"

"Yes, Ma, I have. What about it?"

"Well you know she is Catholic. You're not serious about her, are you?"

Laughing, Paul said, "Don't worry, she's the best hoofer in Brockville. I just enjoy dancing with her."

Martha studied him. His face reddened. Her stomach knotted, she knew he had lied but like Ludwig, her son had a strong will. She knew it would do no good to tell him to quit seeing her. Martha hoped he would soon tire of her and start dating a nice Protestant gal.

During the next three months Paul continued seeing Kathleen. When they were apart he couldn't stop thinking about her. He loved her laugh, her scent, and on the dance floor they entered their own private world. Paul had to tell his brother how he felt about her. They ate lunch together at the brewery and were sitting on the edge of the loading dock. Paul began, "You can't believe how exhilarating it is to dance with Kathleen."

Robert looked at Paul not saying anything. Envious of Paul's relationship with her he wished he could find a similar woman. He'd dated most of the girls in Brockville, but none compared with Kathleen. Robert had often thought about his brother's good fortune.

Robert sighed.

"How about letting me take Kathleen out to the next dance?"

"What do you mean?"

"How about trading places, she will never know."

"Why should I?"

"I'll give you my next month's wages from the brewery."

Paul smirked and punched Robert's shoulder.

"All right bro. Just don't take advantage of the situation."

At the dance Kathleen completely captivated Robert. He smiled all the time and Kathleen reciprocated.

"Paul, you seem to be enjoying tonight."

"Yes, I am. Its like we're dancing for the first time."

During the evening, Paul danced with many girls. When Robert and Kathleen passed him on the way out, Paul winked at Robert and said, "Remember, bro."

Robert walked Kathleen home and then suggested sitting on the porch swing. After swinging for a few minutes, Robert reached out and put his arms around Kathleen, drawing her close. Kissing her caused an electric shock to course through him. Kathleen began responding but then she put her hands against his chest and pushed him away.

"You're Robert!" she gasped.

Robert grinned sheepishly and said, "How did you know?"

Her chest heaving, Kathleen replied, "I just did. You can tell Paul I don't ever want to see him again."

As she said this she jumped up and ran to the door and jerked it open.

Following her, Robert yelled, "Wait."

Kathleen slammed the door in his face.

It took Paul a week of apologizing, cajoling, and pleading with Kathleen before she'd go out with him again.

On April 6th, 1917, two weeks later, Woodrow Wilson and the congress declared war on Germany. Paul and Robert waited three days before enlisting. Prior to leaving for basic training, Paul asked Kathleen to marry him. Herman Darling, a justice of the peace, married them in a private ceremony. They chose Robert and Gretchen for their witnesses.

Martha saw them coming down the sidewalk strolling arm and arm. She went to the front door and stood waiting. As she looked at them, her stomach churned and she tasted bile.

When they reached the front steps, Paul picked Kathleen up and bounded up the steps.

"Ma, I'd like you to meet my wife."

Martha stepped back and said, "You're not bringing her in my house."

She closed the door and locked it.

In June of 1918, the American forces were assigned by the French command to man some of the trenches. Paul and Robert had shipped out to France in the summer of 1917, and their unit had been one of those chosen to enter the line near Chateau Thierry.

As they approached the front on the second, they heard the German artillery and the French guns responding.

When they got to the forward trench the smells became over-whelming, a combination of body odor, cordite, decaying animal and plant matter. Sliding down the sides of the trench into the bottom, their feet became immersed in foot-deep mud.

It took Sergeant Hans Mueller an hour to cross over the Marne and approach the allied trenches. He had started the war on the eastern front. Hans had proven to be a good soldier and a natural leader. Rapidly promoted to sergeant, he had the respect and admiration of his men. Wounded in the leg in October 1916, he returned home to his wife and two boys for a month while he convalesced. Returned to the eastern front after mending, he transferred to the western front after the treaty of Brest Litovsk. In June of 1918 the Germans were staging a massive offensive. This night his lieutenant wanted him to capture a soldier for questioning. His muddy, sweat soaked uniform clung to his body. Dark, with no moon, he could barely see. It was close to midnight when he neared the French line. He stopped when he heard voices.

"Kathleen is really a wonderful wife."

"I know she is, Paul."

Mueller's eyes widened. Making a quick decision, he leaped to his feet and holding his Mauser slanted down, he dropped into the trench. His bayonet sliced into Paul, entering Paul's body below his breastbone. It ended up poking out his back

When Mueller dropped into the trench Robert froze.

Placing his right boot against Paul, Mueller yanked hard but his bayonet didn't budge.

Robert screamed "You bastard" and raising the butt of his Springfield swung at Mueller.

Mueller's bayonet came free from Paul with a sucking sound. Swinging his Mauser around to shoot Robert, he saw the butt coming too late. His yell of "*Gott im Him*… was cut off in mid-word as Robert's stock crashed into his skull. The German fell to the ground.

Robert yelled, "You bloody Hun", and started kicking the dead man. Finally stopping, his breath coming in gasps, he tossed his rifle aside. Falling to his knees, he wrapped his arms around his brother, cradling him. Paul looked into Robert's eyes and managed to whisper, "Please take care of Kathleen." Then his body went limp.

Robert ignored the stench of blood and human excrement. He sat for a long time holding and rocking his brother. Laying the body gently down, he made his decision. Removing Paul's dog tags and billfold, he replaced them with his own.

After the battle of Chateau Thierry the army removed Paul's body along with hundreds of others. They buried them all in a French cemetery forty miles outside of Paris.

A week after Paul's death his parents received the official telegram. *The department of the army regrets to inform you that your son, Robert Metzger, was killed in action on June second in France stop.* Never the same again, Martha, lost her lust for life. When Ludwig informed his co-workers of his son's sacrifice they bowed their heads and silently stood for five minutes in honor of Robert.

After his shift Dennis went to Paul and Kathleen's house and told his sister. "Robert was killed in France on June 2nd. Martha and Ludwig received the telegram today."

Kathleen sank into a chair, chastising herself for feeling glad that it wasn't Paul. She decided she had to attempt to see Ludwig and Martha and offer her sympathy. The next morning she hesitantly approached their house. She knocked on the door. Listening, she heard no sound. Biting her lip, she knocked harder. Sounds of footsteps approached and the door swung open. Kathleen gasped. Martha, her hair unkempt with dark circles under her eyes, raised a shaking hand to her mouth. She stared at Kathleen with her blood shot orbs.

"Yes?"

"Oh, Martha, I'm so sorry about Robert."

For a second Kathleen thought Martha would close the door, but then she reached out and grabbed Kathleen, holding her in a fierce embrace. The two women stood rocking and crying for five minutes and then Martha took her hand and led her into the house. She cried out, "Ludwig, come and see who is here."

Robert fought in a number of engagements; gassed during one of the last battles, when the armistice went into effect he was in a French hospital. He returned to the US in the spring of 1919 and was discharged in Chicago. Catching a train the next morning, he arrived in Brockville late in the afternoon. As he approached Paul and Kathleen's house, he worried about Kathleen's reaction.

Entering through the front door, he yelled out, "Anyone home?"

Hearing his voice, Kathleen came running from the kitchen and grabbing him around the neck started kissing and hugging him, sobbing and laughing between busses. Robert returned her kisses as a warm feeling surged through him.

Suddenly she broke free. A cold hand grabbed his heart and started squeezing. Looking directly into his eyes, Kathleen smiled and said, "Welcome home, Paul." Then she started to waltz him around their living room.

Her thoughts returning to the present, Kathleen reached out and touched the coffin. As she did she bowed her head and prayed, "*Sleep well Robert, yes I knew when you returned home from Europe you'd taken Paul's place but I couldn't bring myself to say anything. These roses are for both of you; I never got to France to place one on Paul's grave. I am looking forward to our reunion in heaven. My dance card is full, but you two are the only ones on it.*"

Placing the two identical roses on the casket, Kathleen turned around and walked back to her car.

War Memorial

Hearing a snap, Tim jerked his head up and stared at the underbrush. Thick and lush, it made seeing anyone approaching difficult. His pulse hammered in his ears and sweat trickled down his back. Dreaming about his mother's flapjacks seconds before, he still saw the stack. The twig had snapped as he started pouring syrup over them.

In the field three hundred yards behind him the Minnesota 4th and 5th regiments were spread out, their tents lined up like rows of corn in a field. He knew Sergeant Driscoll and the boys were counting on him for protection. Driscoll, a foul mouthed Irishman with a ruddy face and massive forearms, bullied his troops. He went easy on Tim, though, because he consistently hit the mark at 100 yards in practice drills, making him the best shot in the 5th regiment.

Tim joined up to kill as many Rebs as possible. A small wiry boy with a serious demeanor, he constantly talked about wanting to charge ahead to engage the enemy. His messmates had nicknamed him Little Bull.

The sky continued to lighten which allowed him to distinguish individual shapes. He cocked his head, straining to hear any sounds. On his right a whippoorwill called in a bunch of pin oaks and directly ahead a group of turkeys clucked and purred.

Hearing a faint scratching sound, Tim brought his musket up and snuggled it against his shoulder. The smooth stock pressed against his cheek; he loved the reassuring feeling he got from it.

Calling, "Thief, thief, thief," a blue jay burst from the cover on his left. An icy shiver started at his scalp and coursed through him. He thought he saw movement and a shadowy form. Tim swung his muzzle over to where the bird had just left. Putting the front bead of his musket in the middle of the shadow, he cocked the hammer and squeezed the trigger. A cloud of smoke wrapped the breach, obscuring his view. As it drifted away, Tim saw leaves shaking where he'd shot. The form had disappeared.

Tremors raced up and down his backbone, but he still remembered his drilling. Reaching into his pouch, he pulled out a paper cartridge and bit off its end. Pouring the powder granules down the barrel with a trembling hand, he shoved the Minnie ball in. With his ramrod, he tamped the bullet home and then slipped the primer over the nipple. After a few minutes, the sounds of the forest and his heart rate returned to normal.

The leaves rustled behind him and he shouldered his musket and swung it around. His bead came to rest in the middle of Sergeant Driscoll's chest. Driscoll's eyes widened.

"Easy, boyo," he growled.

Lowering his weapon, Tim exclaimed, "I think I got a Reb, sergeant."

"You think so? Where?"

"Over to the left, behind those bushes."

"Well, we'll just wait and see if any more show up."

For twenty minutes, they heard the occasional rustling of leaves, birdcalls from the bushes, and faint turkey clucks from the flock Tim scattered when he shot. The camp began to stir, the sounds of metal clanking and men swearing and coughing came on the breeze. Smells of smoke and cooking salt pork drifted over to them. Tim salivated.

"Well, let's see if you got one."

They moved through the undergrowth, holding their muskets ready. Tim's heart pounded against his chest. They both spotted the boots at the same time. The Reb lay on his back, his eyes gleaming. His shot had caught the man in the middle of the chest and the body rested in a pool of congealing blood. Tim paled and stopped.

"Relax," Sergeant Driscoll commanded.

Tim wrenched his gaze away and looked at the underbrush.

"Cover me; I'm going to search old Johnny."

"Yes, Sergeant."

Sergeant Driscoll knelt and patted the man's clothes.

He looked back at the body; his stomach churned.

Sergeant Driscoll pulled a small Bible from the man's breast pocket; its black leather cover worn dull in spots and the gold leaf on the upper right hand page edges worn away. Opening it, he read out loud, "Ethan Bremmer. Baptized April 23, 1831"

"Looks like Ethan was a Christian."

Pulling a letter from the same pocket, Driscoll unfolded it and read out loud.

"Dearest Emily,

We are stationed in Corinth. Rumor has it that the Yankees will attack any day now.

I hope you and the younguns are getting along fine. You shouldn't have any trouble this summer because the garden will supply you with fresh vegetables. You can kill one of our hogs in the fall to carry you through the winter. My mouth is starting to water now just thinking on those delicious hams. I hope this fracas is over with soon so I can return to you and our farm.

We don't have it too bad. The other morning, Frank Larson, he is an Alabama boy in my company, got ahold of some real coffee. We brewed it up and it sure tasted good.

Well, the company commander has just come in, I'll write more later.

Your loving husband,

Ethan."

Driscoll slipped the Bible and letter into his pouch and searched Ethan's jacket. Inserting his hand into the second pocket, he grunted, and withdrew a watch. He held it by its chain; it swung back and forth;

the case glinting in the sun.

"Lookie here, I think you deserve this, take it."

He hesitated, but finally took the proffered timepiece and slipped it into his tunic.

"Thanks, Sergeant."

Beginning to look through Ethan's pants, Driscoll found a small folding knife. He slipped it into his own pocket.

Grinning, Driscoll said, "I'll take the Bible and letter to Captain Boyle. Maybe he can make use of them. Well, lets get back to camp. I see they sent out Billy Gardener to take over your post."

Back at his tent, Tim found Eric Jacobson sitting cross-legged in front of a smoldering fire, holding a small frying pan. A piece of salt pork sizzled and bubbled, giving off a delicious aroma. Eric looked like a Swede, blond, big boned, with fair skin. His uniform rode up on his wrists and ankles.

"This here salt pork is just about ready. I imagine you're real hungry."

Eric and he had joined up together from Freeborn County. They'd known each other for a couple of years; Eric didn't call Tim Little Bull like the other members of C Company. The Jacobson's farm was on the south side of Freeborn Lake and Tim lived a couple of miles north of the village of Freeborn. They'd met in the general store and hit it off from the first. The Jacobson's had come to the county in 1857 from Connecticut, Tim's family, the Duncans, had arrived a year later.

"I kilt me a Reb, Eric."

Eric's eyebrows shot up. "No! Darn, I hope we see some fighting soon so I can kill one."

"Look what Sergeant Driscoll gave me; he took it off the Reb's body."

Tim held up the pocket watch.

Taking it, Eric exclaimed, "Ain't that something. Lookie here, Tim, the case is inscribed"

Tim examined the watch; the engraving read "From Emily to Ethan, 1858." A dull ache started in his chest, but the timepiece felt good lying in his palm, the case as smooth as a polished stone. He put it back in his pocket, liking its heft.

Tim sat down. "Let me have some of that meat you been frying."

After eating, he decided to write a letter home.

"Dear folks,

We are in Mississippi. It's real hot here not like back in Minnesota. We haven't seen much action yet, but I believe it will happen soon.

I was on guard duty last night and shot a rebel. I feel pretty sad about it. His name was Ethan Bremmer and he had a wife named Emily and some kids. He was a farmer just like us. Sergeant Driscoll searched the body and found a pocket watch. He gave it to me. It sure is a wonder, it seems to keep real good time. I showed it to Eric and he thought it was something.

Tell Tom not to join the army. He should stay and help at home.
Your loving son,
Tim

Putting the letter in his pocket, he decided to post it later. He crawled into his tent and lay down. His mind kept returning to the vision of Ethan, his sightless eyes staring blankly. Every few minutes he turned over, trying to find a comfortable position. Finally, he fell into a fitful sleep.

Sergeant Driscoll barked out, "Get ready to move, boyo, we're marching tonight."

Tim groaned awake. A sour smell assaulted his nostrils, and he grimaced when he realized it was his own odor.

After marching all night, Tim and Eric found themselves looking at Corinth on the morning of May 25th. Nauseated, Tim couldn't remain still. They soon would be forming up and advancing on the Rebels. Thundering cannons boomed behind them; they watched as

shells landed among the Confederates. Rebels scurried to put batteries in place. The gray uniformed men were two hundred yards away
and some were taking pot shots at the union line. Standing up for a
better view, Tim started to point something out to Eric when a marks-
man spotted him and raising his musket, fired.

Yelling, "Watch out," Eric tried pulling him down, but the ball
caught Tim in the neck. Falling to the ground, he gripped his throat,
blood spurting out between his fingers. He stared at Eric, his eyes
wild, struggling to speak. Only a garbled sound emerged. Reaching
into his jacket pocket with a shaking palm, Tim withdrew Ethan's
pocket watch and handed it to Eric. Eric grabbed it and thrust it into
his jacket pocket. Taking Tim's hand, he cried out, "Oh, God, please
don't die."

Welling tears clouded Eric's eyes, his heart beat rapidly. The smell
of blood caused his stomach to convulse. His seventeen-year-old
friend's eyes became glassy and his grip loosened. He felt no more
pressure. Eric let Tim's hand drop and sobbed.

After the battle they buried Tim's body in the Corinth Cemetery.
Captain Boyle sent his letter to his folks.

Eric came to believe the watch offered him protection. Before any
of the fights he participated in he would take it out and roll it around
in his hand, feeling its smoothness, its weight. Looking skyward, he
would think about Tim, and what happened at Corinth. At night he
placed it near his head so he could hear it. When it rained or snowed,
he always made sure it remained dry. Eric fought in many battles and at
the siege of Vicksburg; he endured the constant barrage of heavy can-
non. He sat on the ground, his hands over his ears, as a nearby battery
fired shell after shell. After the battle, he held the watch up to his ear.
He took it down, and watched the minute hand move forward. Tears
welled in his eyes and he slipped it into his pocket. The ringing in his
ears continued unabated, and when he awoke each morning, he placed
the watch next to his ear. One day when he held it up, he smiled. From

then on he could again hear his messmates talking around the fire and the camp music. He would sit, listening, his eyes glistening, thinking about Tim and home.

After the war, he returned to Freeborn. When working in the fields, he couldn't hear bird calls or spring peepers like he used to, but the warm sunshine on his face and the smell of new mown hay were as strong as ever. On hikes over the pastures and woods of his land, he would roll the watch around in his hand. Sometimes he caught a faint odor of frying salt pork and wood smoke and he would smile.

Eric didn't talk about his wartime experiences with his family or friends, and he didn't often attend church, because his neighbors always asked him about the watch. "That is a mighty fine looking time-piece, where did you get it?"

"I got it from a friend at Corinth."

If someone wanted to see it, he handed it over and waited. After studying it, they invariably asked who Emily and Ethan were. He always sighed and responded, "I don't know."

Through the years the watch remained in the family, passed down to the oldest son of each generation. His great grandson Eric, who was named in honor of his great grandfather, currently owned it.

This Friday morning Eric sat sipping his coffee, reading the most recent issue of the *Freeborn Frisbee*. He lived in Stillwater, but grew up in Freeborn. Reading the *Frisbee* was better than reading the *Minneapolis Tribune* anyway because of the Iraq news.

Pulling out his watch, he saw it was 8:00. The old relic didn't keep good time, but it still ran. The worn case had exposed copper edges, the silver plating long ago worn off, but it still had the original dial, scratched but solid. Eric always wondered who Emily and Ethan were.

He read with interest an article about Albert Lea building a War Memorial at the court house to honor Freeborn County veterans of past wars. *Maybe I'll contact them about my great grandfather,* he considered.

A couple of weeks later, Eric and his wife Elaine visited the Freeborn County museum to find out more about his great grandfather.

At the museum, they met Joan, a big woman with a ready smile, who said she would be glad to help. She took them to a back room where a grey-haired man and woman sat at a table perusing various papers.

"This is Mr. and Mrs. Benjamin Greer, they're here doing research on Mrs. Greer's great uncle."

Eric extended his hand and said, "Pleased to meet you, this is my wife Elaine and I'm Eric Jacobson."

"Same here, this is my wife Gladys and I'm Ben Greer. So you're here doing research?"

"Yes, my great grandfather fought in the Civil War, his name was Eric Jacobson; he was in the Minnesota 5th.

Gladys, a diminutive women with black hair and lively blue eyes, exclaimed, "Really, my great uncle, Tim Duncan, served in the 5th. He mentions an Eric in a letter sent home after he was killed at the battle of Corinth, Mississippi. Would you like to read it?"

His heart accelerated, smiling, he answered, "Yes"

Gladys handed him the letter. After reading it, Eric gave it back.

"Would you like to see the watch your great uncle got?" With a trembling hand, Eric offered it to her.

A week later, Eric, purchased a brick to be placed at the War Memorial in honor of his great grandfather. It would be inscribed with his great grandfather's name, military branch, and service dates. The Greers received a free brick since her great uncle was killed in action.

It took three months to complete the monument. At the dedication, when the main speakers finished, Eric was called to the dais. Gladys and Ben Greer sat in the first row. He called them forward; they stood by him while he told the story of his great grandfather and the watch. Halfway through he stopped, pressed his lips together, and stared at the sky. His great grandfather's spectral hand from one hundred and fifty-three years ago had reached out and touched him. After a couple of minutes, he resumed speaking. Finishing with a flourish, he said, "Now I would like to present this to Gladys. I think it belongs in her family more than it does ours."

Handing the watch to her, he stepped back and applauded with the crowd.

Afterward, when Gladys and Benjamin drove home, Gladys asked her husband.

"So, do you think we can locate Ethan Bremmer's descendants?"

Lotto

Ted awoke with a start. Ridges of the crumpled damp sheet dug into his body. Totally black out, the weekend wasn't over yet. Glancing at the glowing red numerals on the clock radio, he read 3:21. Since his Lasik surgery, he saw at a distance and only required glasses for reading. They'd warned him scar tissue could prevent them from operating again. He gambled his eyes would remain the same.

Ted had dreamed about his father who had died two months ago. His old man had earned a comfortable six figure salary when he'd retired. His mom and dad wintered in Florida every year and took many trips to Vegas. They both enjoyed gambling but their losses were never large. Sarah, Ted's mom, favored the slots while his dad always sat at the black jack table. His dad frequently bought lottery tickets, especially when the pot rose. The state promoted it in the paper, on the TV, and over the radio. His mom had died five years earlier of stomach cancer, and his dad had a difficult time dealing with her death. However, he continued gambling. When he'd moved into a nursing home two years ago, he and some of his buddies always took the bus tour to the casinos.

Ted recalled his dream. In it his dad had told him, "I want you to buy a lottery ticket with numbers based on the birthdays of family members. Use mine, Jill's, your three kids, and your birthday for the power ball. You can't lose." The current jackpot now totaled over two hundred million.

Ted looked over at his wife. She slept soundly; her chest rising and falling rhythmically. Jill came from a broken home. Her dad, a compulsive gamer, had gambled away their home and his marriage.

After the divorce, Jill and her two siblings had it tough. Their mother worked as a waitress and they were always short on money. Jill had gone to college and gotten an education degree. To help pay for her tuition, she'd followed in her mom's foot steps, working as a waitress while attending school. She'd financed want she couldn't pay for by taking out student loans. She hated gambling. When she'd married Ted she made him promise he'd never get involved with it.

Ted slipped out of bed. He went to the wall switch and flipped on the light. Jill slept through anything.

He thought, *I'm going to write the numbers down before I forget.*

Opening the middle dresser drawer, he rummaged around until he found a ballpoint. Looking at the top of the dresser, he spotted an envelope. He took the letter and wrote the birthdays on its blank backside. He heard the bed squeak. Turning around, he saw Jill turn over. To his surprise, she looked up at him through sleep swollen eyes and said, "What are you doing, Ted?"

"Nothing, go back to sleep."

A sigh escaped his lips when he saw her eyes close. She resumed sleeping. His heart returned to its normal beating.

After finishing his shift at the hospital on Monday, he stopped at a Super America store to fill up. When he went into pay he'd waited in line for a long time. When he got to the counter he handed the freckled faced clerk who sported an ear stud, two twenties and the envelope with the birthday dates on it.

"Gas on six, give me a power ball with those numbers on it, please."

"That's $26.50 out of forty for gas and $1.00 for the ticket."

The clerk entered the numbers, generated the ticket, and handed it to him with his change.

"Do you want the envelope back?"

"No, toss it"

"Thank you, have a nice day."

Ted shifted from foot to foot in front of the counter, his face started getting warm. He thought, *I've never bought any tickets before. Jill is going to kill me if she finds out.*

Seeing Ted in front of the counter, the clerk said, "Anything else?"

"Give me five more power ball numbers, please"

He'd scribbled his name on the back of the birthday ticket. In the dream his dad told him to make sure that he signed immediately after purchasing it to insure he would win.

Coming out of the exit, he almost bumped into a tall, muscular young guy.

"Excuse me."

Grinning, the guy said, "That's alright, fella."

Ted put the two tickets in his billfold and drove home.

"Hi, hon."

"How'd your shift go today?"

"Fine, did we get any mail?"

Ted, a LPN for the local Stillwater hospital, worked the 9:00 AM to 5:00 PM shift. He went into the bedroom to change his clothes since he still had on his whites. Taking the tickets out of his wallet, he put them in the paperback lying on the dresser.

Jill always did the grocery shopping on Tuesday morning. She'd get up early before he and the kids were up and go to Cub. Old fashioned, she paid cash and frequently went through Ted's billfold to get money. This Tuesday morning, she arose at her usual hour. She turned on the light, Ted slept through anything; his soft snoring continued unabated. Going over to the dresser, she picked up his billfold and took out six twenty dollar bills. The rich odor of new leather filled her nostrils and she smiled. She'd gotten it for his birthday.

Placing it back down, her eye focused on the author's name of Ted's current book. It was Dan Brown.

They were reading "The DaVinci Code" in their group at church. Picking it up, Jill started thumbing through it. Two slips of paper fell out. Picking up one of them, her eyes widened and her hand started shaking.

A dull ache started in her chest. She ripped the ticket up and reached for the other. It had landed with its backside up. Grabbing it, Jill started to tear it up, but stopped when she saw Ted's signature.

Opening Ted's top drawer, Jill threw the ticket in.

It caught against a handkerchief and fell down behind the packed drawer when she slammed it shut.

Millions of tickets were being sold in the states with power ball. One buyer in Minnesota besides Ted was Jim Evans, the guy Ted narrowly missed bumping into at the convenience store. On Monday morning Jim had listened to 109. In between songs the announcers promoted the Power Ball.

"Yes sir, Rockers, the jackpot is now a cool 210 million."

Jim moved to Stillwater after he'd gotten a job at Medtronics. He'd graduated from Purdue three years ago with a Master's degree in electrical engineering. All his family still lived in Indiana. Single, he enjoyed the night life and dated many girls. His current girl friend loved gambling and had told him to buy a power ball ticket.

On their date last night, she started talking about the lottery and what she would do if she won. Jim asked her, "Do you know what the odds are against winning?"

Marcy pouted, "I know it isn't good, but someone has to win Maybe it will be me."

"I will buy one tomorrow. If I win I'll share the winnings with you."

When he stopped for gas after work he bought one. Going into the Stillwater Super America store he'd bumped into a guy dressed all in white. The guy was focused on something in his hand and walked right into him. When he'd gone in the store to pay, he purchased a single ticket. In his mind Marcy's pouting lips curved upwards.

Jim asked the clerk, "When is the next drawing?"

On 10:00 Wednesday evening Jill and Ted sat watching TV. The kids were in bed. They had satellite and taking the remote Ted changed to Channel 45.

"Why did you change the channel, Ted?"

"Because they broadcast the Power Ball drawing."

"Why do you want to watch that?"

"Because."

Jill got up, walked out of the family room and went into their bedroom. She lay down on the bed to read.

The drawing began. The first white ball's number was 18. The remaining four white balls were selected. Ted sat on the edge of his seat. With each ball he'd inched further forward and his heart rate increased. His wide open glassy eyes reflected the image on the screen. Miniscule moisture droplets covered his upper lip and forehead. They drew the red ball; it was 31. Ted raised his arms over his head, clinching his right hand, he pumped it.

Ted shouted "Jill we're rich."

"What did you say?"

"We're rich!"

Walking into the bedroom, Ted went to the dresser and picked up "Deception Point". He opened it at the book marker.

Setting her book down, Jill said, "It isn't there, Ted."

Jerking around, Ted looked at her; his face drained of color.

"Where is it?"

"I tore one ticket up, but I threw the one with your name on it into your junk drawer. Is that the one you want?"

"Do you know how much that ticket is worth?"

"No, and I don't care."

"Only about 200 million."

"So, I don't believe you've won."

Jill got up and walked out into the family room.

Ted listened to Jill's receding foot steps. He grabbed his junk drawers handle and opened it. Holding his hand on top of the mess; he pulled it all the way out. Looking over the piles top, he didn't see it. He started taking items out, throwing them on the bed. When he'd emptied the drawer, he still hadn't found it. His head ached and his chest felt cold. He went through everything again. No ticket.

He yelled, "Jill, come here."

"What?"

Ted yelled out a lot louder, "Get in here."

Jill appeared in the door.

"Are you sure you put the ticket in my drawer."

"Yes. Lower your voice or you're going to wake the kids. You can never find anything, here let me look."

Jill went through the scattered items.

"I know I put it in here."

Ted threw up his arms and snarled "Great, I win the mega jackpot and you lose the ticket."

"You have too much crap. Maybe it fell down behind when I shut the drawer."

Ted looked at her wide-eyed, going over he jerked open the drawer and tilted it sharply downward.

One of the draw guides broke with an audible crack. Ted yanked the drawer out. Bending down, he peered in the dark opening.

"Get me a flashlight."

Jill's eyebrows shot up. "Anything else master?"

"Just shut the fuck up and get me the flashlight."

Jill returned in a few minutes and handed the flashlight to Ted. He turned it on and the feeble yellowish light barely illuminated the opening.

Shaking his head, Ted said, "You've let the kids play flashlight tag again haven't you. Do we have any batteries?"

"Yes, I'll go get some."

Jill handed him the batteries.

Ted aimed the bright beam into the opening. At first he didn't see anything, but then his eye caught the corner of the ticket that stuck up in back. He reached in and extracted it.

"Fantastic."

Ted looked at the numbers. The power ball was 13.

A chill shot through his body. His hand holding the ticket shook.

He thought, "*I don't fucking believe this. The kid at the convenience store must have transposed the numerals when he entered it.*"

While Jill and Ted looked for Ted's ticket, Jim Evans sat staring at his computer screen. The numbers, including the power ball number, all matched his ticket. Getting up, he grabbed his cell phone from the kitchen. He dialed Marcy's number, but no one answered so he tried again a half and hour later but still got no answer. Going into his bedroom, he undressed and climbed into bed where he lay staring at the ceiling thinking about his winnings. His mind raced and he turned from side to side. The night lasted forever, and when he managed to nod off, the alarm jangled him awake. Getting up, he threw on his clothes. Slightly nauseated and dizzy, he surprised himself. He had no hunger pangs. Without taking time to eat, he left for the Lotto center in Roseville to claim his prize.

As he was driving over, he called his office on his cell phone "Hello Brenda, I won't be coming in today, I've decided to take a day of vacation."

Putting down the phone, he applied the brake and stopped for the red light. It turned green and he headed across the intersection. He never saw the car on the left. The driver tried to make it through on yellow.

Jim never wore a seat belt; his head slammed into the windshield.

Fissures radiated outward in the glass as his head crashed down onto the dashboard.

They brought the two victims in on Ted's shift. The woman had a ruptured spleen, two broken ribs, a broken leg, and a gash on her forearm. She'd be sore for awhile, but would fully recover. The man had a severe head injury. In a coma, he probably would never again be conscious. Even if he did regain consciousness, there was certain to be brain damage.

Ted took Jim's clothes to his room and went to the closet to hang them up. As he put the shirt on a hanger, he noticed the lottery ticket in the breast pocket.

Reaching in the pocket, he withdrew it and looked at the number.

Ted trembled as sweat beaded his forehead.

Ted reached for his billfold and withdrew his ticket. He held Jim's between his lips.

He put his ticket in the shirt and placed Jim's in his billfold.

Ted took the cash payment. He received 68.7 million after taxes. No one ever cashed his. He quit the hospital, and Jill and he traveled a lot. They bought a house in Arizona and spend the winters there.

After Jim recovered, they placed him in a Stillwater nursing home and later transferred him to one in Indiana. His mother visited him quite often, sitting beside the bed holding his hand.

Jim's mother sighed as she looked out the window of the Indianapolis Good Samaritan nursing home. She opened the envelope. Jim always received a cashier's check for $50,000 from an anonymous person on the first of each month.

Choices

Looking at the bills, she saw the clerk had given her a twenty and four ones. "Excuse me; I think you gave me the wrong change."

The young clerk said, "Oh yes, I must have reached in the wrong compartment."

Giving the twenty back, Susan said, "It is easy to do."

The clerk took the twenty and handed Susan a ten. "Thank you very much. I would have been short."

"You're welcome"

Susan buttoned her coat and left the store. She strolled down the sidewalk. Her foot slid on an icy patch and she looked down. Lying on the cement was a small package. She stooped down and picked it up, turning it over as she did. On a white label she read, *Allen Stoddard, Nelson's Jewelry Store, 165 South Main St, Beddington, Iowa.* He had recently taken over his father-in-law's store. She shoved the package into her purse, walked to her car, and drove home.

Entering the house, she placed the box on the kitchen table. After hanging up her coat she returned to examine it. Noticing its hinged lid, she carefully pried on the flap, managing to open it without damage. As she slid her fingers in, she felt something soft. She removed it. Staring at the blue bag, she massaged its bottom, it held some hard objects.

She opened the sack and dumped the pieces out on the table. She gasped. The contents sparkled and twinkled under the kitchen light. They were diamonds. Trembling, she sat mesmerized. When Susan and Jim married, he bought her a small diamond ring. She told him

"It is lovely. I will always cherish it."

A couple of weeks ago her best friend Marge, had received a large diamond from her husband. At their church circle meeting Marge flashed it around. Everybody exclaimed how beautiful it was.

"How do you like my ring, Susan?"

"It is fantastic."

Marge had fat stubby fingers. Her own hands were beautiful.

She heard rumbling in the garage. Susan froze. An icy feeling gripped her. Jim was home. She scooped up the stones and put them back in the bag. Stuffing it back into the box, she got up and ran across the kitchen. She jerked open a cabinet drawer and threw the package in.

Jim called out, "I'm home."

She heard footsteps in the family room. Slamming the drawer, she leaned against the counter. Jim entered the kitchen.

"Hi, babe. What are you cooking? I don't smell anything."

"I forgot about supper. Since Jessica is at Mom's, why don't we go out tonight?"

"Sounds good to me. Where do you want to go?"

The next morning when Jim got out of bed he said, "Aren't you going to church today?"

"I don't feel well, why don't you go without me. Remember that you have to pick up Jessica."

After he left she listened for the garage door to open. She heard the car back out. Jumping out of bed, she ran to the window and saw Jim drive away.

Walking into the kitchen, she went to the drawer and took out the box. She went over to the table and scattered the diamonds on it. One of the larger stones caught her eye and she examined it. It sparkled under the light and she saw blues, greens, reds, and yellows. To her it was the prettiest thing she had ever seen. Her pupils dilated as tiny beads of sweat popped out on her brow. Her heart thumped against her chest. She thought, *too bad I have to take the diamonds back to Allen.*

Already bald, Allen wore thick glasses which magnified his eyes. Whenever they met, his eyes shifted from her face to her breasts. Allen and Susan went to high school together; he had never been popular and had not dated much in school. Susan was an attractive blue-eyed blond. Her armpits always became wet and her lips whitened when they talked. She always wondered what his wife, Jill, thought about her husband. Gathering up the diamonds, she put them back in the drawer. She walked back to the table. With a trembling hand, she picked up the one she had selected. She almost dropped it; she tightened her grip until her knuckles turned white.

On Monday she went to Stoddard's jewelry with the package. Handing it to Allen, she said, "I found this lying on the sidewalk on Saturday. Your store was closed so I took it home."

Allen stared at her with his oversized eyes. "Thanks. Did you open it?"

"No. What is in it?"

Allen opened the box and dumped the diamonds on the counter.

Susan trembled. "I had no idea. They are so beautiful."

"I appreciate what you did. Why don't you pick out one of these amethyst necklaces?"

"I couldn't do that."

She went outside and leaned up against the building. Bile rose up into her throat. Placing her arms across her midsection, she squeezed.

On Wednesday she drove over to Parkington. Marge's husband had purchased her ring there. Going into the store, she stopped and looked at the diamond rings.

"Can I help you, Miss?"

Susan jumped back. Looking at the man, she saw laugh wrinkles surrounding his eyes and mouth. She relaxed. "No, yes, I mean I am not here to buy anything. I want to have a ring made."

Reaching into her pocket, she took out the box, opened it, and held it out.

"That is a magnificent stone. Where did you get it?"

"From my elderly aunt. Could you make a ring for me?"

"Yes. What kind of setting do you want?"

"Could you make it look old? I love antique jewelry."

"Yes. Personally I don't like the new styles either.

Taking the stone, he examined it with his eyepiece.

"This is remarkable gem; I'm looking forward to working with it."

Susan got his call a week later.

"The ring is done. I think it turned out beautifully."

She drove over immediately and picked it up. It slid on her finger easier than she expected.

That night when he came home, Jim noticed right away. His brow wrinkled and he said, "Where did you get the ring?"

"I got it from Aunt Bess. I don't think I ever told you about her. She is quite old and wanted me to have it." She hoped he did not detect her tremor.

At church the following Sunday she took the bulletin from Allen. He was ushering this morning. "Beautiful ring, did Jim buy it for you?"

"No, I inherited it." Her heart rate jumped.

Reverend Benson climbed into the pulpit and began his sermon. "Today I would like to talk about honesty. Many people in our congregation consider us good honest Christians. If we were presented with an opportunity to lie or steal something, no matter how small, most people in this congregation would do the right thing. I have faith that you would avoid temptation just as Christ did when the devil tempted him."

Susan labored to breathe. Blackness appeared at the edges of her vision. Her ears buzzed. Darkness closed in and Susan hung her head. She no longer heard what Reverend Benson said.

She felt a hand on her arm and Jim whispered, "What is the matter?"

"I'll be alright, for a minute I felt faint but my head is starting to clear."

Susan did not listen to anymore of the sermon and kept repeating over and over to herself, *I am going to take this ring back tomorrow; I am going to take this ring back tomorrow.*

On the way out she tried to avoid Reverend Benson. However, she found herself boxed in. She stared at his outstretched hand. Taking it, she mumbled," Good sermon" but when he attempted to look her in the eye she pulled away.

"Nice to see you in church, Susan." He turned to the next parishioner in line.

After Jim left to work she went to Nelsons where she saw Allen behind the counter. She said, "Could we go back in your office? I've got something I want to give you."

"Sure, I have been expecting you."

Trailing him into his office, she seated herself in front of his desk. He sat down in his chair, leaned back and put his arms behind his head.

"What did you mean out there, you have been expecting me?"

"I knew you would come in. You want to give back the diamond."

She shuddered. "How did you know?"

"All the diamonds we receive are marked. We have an inventory list. As soon as I saw your ring I knew."

"Can I give it back?" She hated the pleading sound of her voice.

He leaned forward. His lips curled into a lewd grin as his eyes fixed on her chest. "Susan, Susan, Susan, do you know how much it is worth? I would say about $15,000."

"What do you want?"

He said in a husky voice, "You can keep it but let's you and I have a weekly meeting. I will give you $100 a time. What do you say?"

Her face burned and her lips drained of color.

She mumbled, "What if I don't agree?"

"I will tell everyone what you did. Think it over and get back to me."

Susan jumped up and ran out of the office. Going outside, she almost stumbled. Her shoulders slumped and tears flowed down her cheeks. She walked back to her car. On the way home she got an idea. She smiled.

"Hello, Mr. Benson?"

"Yes."

"This is Mrs. Sanders. You recently made a ring for me."

"Yes, I remember. Exquisite stone."

"Would you like to buy it?"

"Maybe, bring it in and we'll discuss it."

Susan drove over to Parkington the next day.

"I will give you $12000 for it Mrs. Sanders."

"It isn't worth more?"

"No, that is a fair price."

"Can you pay me right now?"

"Yes, we'll go over to my bank and I'll have them make out a cashiers check."

At the bank the teller asked whom to make the check out to. When she arrived home, Susan dropped the envelope with the check in the mailbox.

In the house she grabbed the phone book and looked under escort services. There were three listed. Selecting the second one, she dialed. A man picked up and said, "Miller Escort Service."

Gracie turned out to be likeable gal. Young, with bad teeth but a cute face and a knockout figure she readily agreed to go along with Susan.

"Hello, Allen?"

"Yes."

"This is Susan. I want to meet you today. I'll be at the Prescot hotel.

"What time?"

"Be there at 2:30." She hung up.

When Allen arrived at the Prescot he asked the desk clerk. "Is there a Mrs. Susan Sanders registered?"

"Yes, but I can't give you her room."

"Would you please call and tell her Allen Stoddard is here."

Allen knocked on the door. It opened

"Come in Allen, I've been waiting for you."

His eyes widened. Susan was dressed in a blue negligee. He stared at her nipples. He swallowed.

"Get undressed, lover boy."

Allen did so in a rush. He almost fell down trying to get out of his pants.

"You get in bed. I have to use the bathroom."

He took his glasses off and crawled in, his heart thumping in his chest and his member rising.

The toilet flushed and Susan called out, "Ready or not here I come. Shut your eyes."

The bed bounced and her warm body molded up against his.

"Oh, Susan."

Allen opened his eyes. They popped wide.

"What the hell, you're not Susan."

"No, I'm not." Gracie giggled.

"Look over this way, Allen."

Allen stared at Susan. She began taking pictures.

After they got dressed Susan told Allen, "I won't let Jill see these photos if you don't tell anyone about the ring."

Allen opened the envelope and a note dropped out. He read,

This is for the diamond; don't let anyone say I don't pay my debts. I'll be down to pick up my amethyst necklace next Thursday.

Susan

Accidental Christmas Meal

Ron watched as the snow approached. It coated the tree leaves and hung like gauze from their crowns. He shifted his butt to relieve the ache, and looked at his watch, only ten minutes left of the season. *No deer this year to fill up my freezer, oh well, Marcie will be glad.* The time crawled by, and he fought looking at his Casio. Finally he gave in and smiled when he saw eleven minutes had passed. He got up and started walking back out, following the well used deer trail.

A half hour later the pickup came into view, and he grinned when he saw Len coming down the trail. *No waiting out in the cold for him to get back and unlock his vehicle tonight.*

"How did you do?"

"I didn't see anything. Boy, it sure is a black night."

Ron opened the door and climbed in. "I guess we'll have to wait for next year."

Len turned the key and backed out of the parking area. "Yeah, this is the second year in a row I haven't got a shot."

As they rode along, they discussed their season, both agreeing that this was one of the worst. When they were close to Benson and home, Len got a call on his cell phone.

"Hello, Barbara?"

"Yeah, we are only a couple of miles out."

"Nah, neither one of us saw anything."

As Len said this, a deer, wraith like, appeared on the side of the road. It stuck its head into their lane and Len braked. Ron watched fascinated as the animal tried to back up, but there were three other deer and they forced it forward. It stuck its head back into their lane and the right front of the pickup smacked into it. "Len yelled, "Son-of-a-bitch."

The pickup shuddered, followed by a thud, Ron saw a glob of something shoot from the deer's head, and then they were by it. Lights from oncoming and trailing cars were strung like glitter beads on a necklace so they couldn't stop.

Ron pointed to the left side of the road. "See that filling station; you have to get gas anyway, pull in there."

Len pulled up to the gas pumps and Ron opened his door. It stopped a third of the way and wouldn't open any further, so he eased through the opening and stepped out. The door had a big dent in it and there was a long crease in the club cab door behind it. When he walked around in front, the headlight dangled from its wires and it no longer had a housing. The fender looked like an accordion where it met the hood.

Len came around the front and grimaced. "Goddamn it, I've only got eight thousand miles on this truck."

"Yeah, too bad you hit the deer."

Len shook his head. "This looks like four thousand worth of damage to me."

"You did the right thing, though; if you would have swerved we'd either have hit a car or gone over the edge of the embankment and ended up in the swamp."

A car, with a small blond woman behind the wheel, pulled in alongside of them. The passenger window rolled down and the gal yelled through the opening, "You guys hit a deer. It is lying back there along side of the road."

The woman leaned over and studied Ron. "Mr. Ferguson?"

"Yeah, Shirley?"

Shirley smiled, "I called the sheriff; he should get here any minute."

Just then a car pulled onto the shoulder not too far away from where they had hit the deer and a bar light on its top started flashing, red, white, and blue.

"There he is now, thanks for calling him."

"Hey, no problem."

"Is Bruce still in Iraq?"

Shirley nodded. "His unit is scheduled to be back in late February."

"He is a deer hunter, right?"

"Yeah, he has gotten one every year, I'm going to miss not having venison this season. I just love the meat and it really helps on grocery bills."

"Well, thanks again. I suppose your mother-in-law is watching the kids."

Shirley nodded. "That is the only way I can get away for awhile. What are you going to do with the deer?"

"We'll go back and gut her and then take it to my place for skinning and butchering."

After Len filled up and paid for the gas they drove back, and parked on a side road near the sheriff's car. The sheriff stood on the shoulder, searching the ditch for the deer with a big flashlight, its beam like a lighthouse beacon.

Ron called from across the road, "You're looking in the wrong place, it's back further."

Len and Ron waited for an open spot in the traffic, then dashed across. Ron motioned for the sheriff to follow him, and started walking back toward where he thought they hit the deer. After going about a quarter mile, the flashlight illuminated the animal; it lay on the embankment about halfway down. The sheriff, a trim middle aged man with a burr cut and freckles asked, "Do you have a knife?"

Ron reached down and unfastened the flap of the sheath on his three bladed knife. "How does this one look?"

The sheriff grinned, "I've got one just like it; you bought it from Cabelas, right?"

"Yup, sure did."

The sheriff held his flashlight on the deer for Ron to gut and afterward went ahead of them as they carried the deer back to the pickup. The sheriff gave Len an accident report form, and told him how to fill it out. They shook his hand, and Len said, "Thanks for all your help."

Marcie, Ron's slightly overweight but good looking wife with gold hoop earrings swinging, stood in the doorway of the garage shaking her head.

"You aren't going to keep all that venison are you?"

Len had just left with his processed and packaged half; at least he would have something to show for their hunt besides a damaged vehicle.

"No, I'm not. I will just keep the tenders and prepare a romantic dinner for us. When I get done here, I will tell you what we are going to do with the rest of it"

Marcie made a face and laughed, "So, you have big plans, huh," and then she shut the door.

Tom, Shirley's oldest boy, opened the door. At ten years old, he stood almost as tall as his old man, and like him, he had a shock of unruly black hair. He wore a Viking jersey with the number four on it.

"Hey Mom, Mr. and Mrs. Ferguson are here."

"Well, invite them in."

"Come on in, my mom's in the kitchen."

"Do you like football?"

"Yeah, my dad got this for my birthday."

Tom turned and motioned for them to follow. Ron picked up the ice chest; Marcie held a bag full of the necessary fixings along with a brightly wrapped bottle of a premium merlot.

They found Shirley feeding one year old Greg, who sat in his highchair banging his spoon on the tray, and flinging his food around. Unlike Tom, he had Shirley's blond hair and blue eyes, his hair and eyebrows now spotted with globs of Tater Tot hot dish. Amber, Shirley's blonde six year old, sat at the table diligently drawing in a note book. Ron glanced over her shoulder and his eyes widened. The clowns were pretty good for a six year old.

"Do you like clowns?"

Amber nodded and continued to concentrate, a crease running down her forehead and her tongue sticking out at the corner of her mouth.

Ron set the ice chest down; Shirley pointed to it and asked, "What's in it?"

"It is your Christmas gift from Marcie and me. Take a look."

When Shirley opened it, she clapped her hands and grinned. "Is this the venison from your road kill?"

"It sure is. Marcie also agreed to cook us Swiss steak for tonight, and let me tell you she is one mean cook. Do you have a bottle opener?

Two hours later the delicious smells of good food filled the kitchen. After they all sat down at the table, Ron raised his glass in a toast. "To Bruce, may he be home this time next year to supply his own venison."

At the door, Shirley hugged both of them. When she released Ron, she said, "Thanks for thinking of us, I know Bruce will really appreciate this. Merry Christmas and Happy New Year, you are both wonderful people."

Donation

The bluish smoke cloud drifted overhead. Tim's eyes hurt and the smell nauseated him. Loud pulsating music blasted from the speakers assailing his eardrums. Gina danced lasciviously and languorously around the pole. Looking at Tim, she winked. The customers hooted and howled.

Only one more shift and then I'm done.

Tim pondered the circumstances that had brought him to work in this degrading place. The downward spiral started after he'd found the billfold. Every Christmas season he worked as a bell ringer for the Salvation Army. He enjoyed standing outside in the cold volunteering since people were so generous. He'd recently heard about an anonymous donor who put a $15000 dollar check in one of the kettles. Tim was envious; he did a lot of charitable work but had little money to donate.

Tim lived in Mountain Rock, Wisconsin a community of seventy five thousand located on the Mississippi River. He was an LPN for the local hospital and his wife Jennifer taught third grade at Lincoln elementary. Their youngest, Tom, finished school last year and had gotten a job as a chemist for 3M in St. Paul. Their oldest, Paula, married last year and Jennifer and he were eagerly awaiting the birth of their first grandchild. Tim and Jennifer attended church regularly and volunteered frequently. They pledged as much money as they were able to during the year. Tim argued with Jen about this since he wanted to give more money to The United Way or the Salvation Army but she remained adamant.

"The church deserves our financial support, Tim, its better to give there than secular charities like United Way or the Salvation Army. We can see where it goes."

The day after working at the bar, Tim stood in front of the Cub grocery store stamping his feet and ringing his bell. Tim was the last bell ringer of the day. He'd stood in one of the doorways to Cub for four hours. The last dona-tors had trouble getting their dollars in and had to work to stuff them in. Every time the door opened the smell of food wafted out from the store's deli and he'd start salivating. One woman gave him a treat, a chocolate mint wrapped in green foil that he'd slipped into a pocket of his apron for enjoying later. Just then, a van with a Salvation Army emblem drove up and stopped right in front of him. It was John, the overseer of the bell ringers.

"Looks like you've got a full kettle here, Tim."

After John drove off, he'd found the wallet lying on the sidewalk in a shadowed corner next to where his friend Dick had rung. Tim reached down and picked it up.

Three hours earlier Brad Lewinsky had walked toward Cub headed for its in house bank.

A Salvation Army bell ringer was standing by the entrance. He'd completely faked the guy out. Coming up to him he reached into his pocket and withdrew his billfold pretending to take out a bill. Extending his closed hand over the kettle he held it there. Turning, the bell ringer looked directly at Brad and started to say "Merry Chris…" and stopped abruptly. He stared wide eyed at Brad's clinched hand with the middle finger extended.

"Merry Christmas to you chump, ha, ha."

Smiling, Brad walked into the store and went over to the bank. Earlier in the week he'd called ahead to make sure they'd have the hundreds for him. He always gave his nieces and nephews each a hundred dollar bill at Christmas. His wife, Lola, and he didn't want any kids but he came from a large family and his brothers and sisters all had packs. His sister Victoria just had her fifth for Christ's sake. This year he'd have to get forty one bills.

Brad had recently received a lot of negative publicity in the local paper. He owned two strip joints and the city council tried to close him down. His picture was printed along side one of the first articles. It was a recent one.

"That is really a good picture of you, Brad."

"Shut up, Lola. You're lucky I married you so you don't have to perform anymore."

Brad's joints were really doing well. He was a multimillionaire. The action by the city council proved to be beneficial, business was booming.

The teller was counting out his money. That is four thousand, four thousand one hundred. Brad liked the looks of the crisp notes. Grabbing the proffered bills he said, "Happy Holidays"

"Happy Holidays to you Mr. Lewinsky."

Taking out his billfold Brad started stuffing the currency in to it while he walked to the exit.

"Ding, ding, ding."

Jesus, they've got another bell ringer at the exit.

He dodged around the bell ringer and at the same time reached around to place the fat wallet into his rear pocket. Just as he did an old woman ran into him with her cart. She was headed over to the kettle to stuff in her tightly clutched crumpled dollar. Distracted he missed his pocket and when he let go, the billfold fell to the sidewalk.

"Ouch"

"Goddam it, woman."

"I'm so sorry. Are you hurt?"

"What do you think?"

"Merry Christmas"

"Ya, ya, Merry Christmas, next time watch where you're going."

Brad's face was hot and he wanted to reach out and strangle the old bitch but he turned abruptly and limped to his car. His Achilles' tendon hurt like hell.

A half-hour after Brad drove off Tim went over to the entrance to see how Dick was doing with his kettle.

"Keeping warm, Dick?"

The wind had come up and the temperature was dropping. Tim was glad he'd thought to bring hand warmers along.

"My hands are a little cold."

"Here take these."

"Did you see Lewinsky?"

"Ya, I did."

"You know what he did?"

Dick told Tim what had happened.

Tim removed the driver's license from its slot and looked at it. Brad Lewinsky's face stared back at him. He looked into the money compartment, and pulled out one of the bills. In its center was Ben Franklin. Removing the wad, he started counting, there were forty one hundred notes plus a five. By the time he finished his hand shook. Stuffing the money back in Tim walked to his car.

Before his shift the next morning he drove out to Lewinsky's river home.

"What a place. They must have to communicate using Walkie Talkies."

Tim stood in front of the massive oak doors. Reaching out his hand he guided it toward the door bell. He placed his finger on its button and started to press. Right before the electrical signal activated the chime, he withdrew his digit. Turning, he walked back down the landscaped walk.

Tim drove downtown and parked in the lot of the Rexall drug store. Getting out, he took out Lewinsky's billfold and pulled out three hundreds. As he approached the bell ringer he folded them up.

"Ding, ding, ding....."

Tim stuffed the bills in the kettle.

"Thank you, Merry Christmas."

"Merry Christmas to you."

He'd gone to all the ringers in town. The last one was at Cub and when he came up he saw that it was his friend Dick. He'd had two hundreds left and he stuffed the folded bills into Dick's pot.

"Merry Christmas, Tim."

"Merry Christmas, Dick. Are you and Ruby going to the candle-light service on Christmas Eve?

He'd sent Lewinsky's billfold to him in the mail. Tim didn't put his return address on the envelope. The Sunday after Christmas Pastor Willis's sermon was on honesty. During the sermon Tim's face became hot and sweat beads popped out on his forehead. Wiping it with his hand he thought, "Maybe what I did wasn't so good."

He continued sweating; it felt as if needles were being inserted into his skin. Jennifer looked at him and whispered, "What's the matter, Tim?"

After his shift on Monday Tim drove out to Lewinsky's house. This time he'd rung the bell. A pretty young blonde woman with a heavily made up face answered the door. Tim smelled her perfume, pleasant but she must have bathed in it.

"Yes?"

"Is Mr. Lewinsky here?"

A man's voice called from the back of the house, "Who is it Lola?"

Lola had taken him into the living room where Lewinsky was sitting. It was a beautiful place. Huge windows faced the river and there was a large fire place on one end of the room. A massive Christmas tree stood in one corner, its top only inches away from the vaulted ceiling. An angel looked down from its top.

Tim went up to Lewinsky and as he did Lewinsky got up and extended his hand. Tim took it and while shaking said, "Hi, my name is Tim Bauer."

Lewinsky's handshake was firm and his palm dry.

"Brad Lewinsky, what can I do for you?"

Tim smelled juniper berries. Lewinsky's blood shot eyes studied him.

"Can we talk in private, Mr. Lewinsky?"

"You can say anything you what in front of Lola, she knows everything."

Lola looked at Lewinsky and arched her eye brow.

"Take a seat, Bauer. Do you want anything to drink?"

"No, thank you."

Lewinsky collapsed back into his chair. Lola stood by him and began to stroke his hairy arm.

Tim swallowed, his mouth was dry and it hurt slightly. "I was the one who found your billfold. Did you get my package in the mail with it?"

"Ya, I did. Do you know anything about my missing money?"

Tim felt his face get hot, again he swallowed; it felt like he had a mouth full of dry sand.

"Yes I do, when I found it there were forty one hundred dollar bills in it."

"Where are they?"

"I put them all in the Salvation Army Kettles."

"Clap"

Lola had clapped her hands together and stood grinning. She started laughing. Lewinsky leaned forward and spat out, "You expect me to believe that?"

Tim felt drops of sweat pop out on his forehead as prickles spread across it.

"Yes."

"You stole the cash and then gave it away?"

"Yes."

Lewinsky just sat and stared at Tim. Finally he said, "What a chump. Do you have a check?"

"We don't have that much money; I can't pay you right now."

"You steal my money, a gift for my family, and now you tell me you can't pay?"

"Yes."

Again Lewinsky sat looking at him for a long time. Lola's smile was still plastered to her face and she winked at Tim.

"Tell you what, Bauer. I won't drag you into court if you work in one of my clubs to pay the money off."

"You want me to work in one of your strip joints?"

"Sure, why not. You're big enough. I need another bouncer."

"What if I don't?"

"Then I'll see you in court."

"Can I let you know tomorrow?"

"Okay, if you show up at the Hill Topper at 7:30PM tomorrow I'll see you then, otherwise like I said it will be before a judge. Do you know how to get there?

After leaving Lewinsky's Tim drove home. Jennifer didn't know anything about this.

"Why are you late, Tim? The meat loaf and potatoes are dried out. Next time call if you're going to be late."

During the meal Tim told her all about what had happened and what Lewinsky proposed. Halfway through telling her he decided.

After he finished Jennifer said, "What are you going to do?"

"Work as a bouncer."

Jennifer's face colored

"You're not really are you?"

"We don't have the money to pay him."

"Oh, Tim, how could you?"

Tears welled up in Jennifer's eyes and she started crying. Tim's stomach turned over and he got up and came over to her. He started to put an arm around her shoulder.

"Don't touch me; I knew the Salvation Army wasn't any good."

He'd gone out to the Hill Topper the following evening. At five dollars an hour it took a long time to pay Lewinsky back. During his time there Jennifer came to accept it but still harbored a little resentment.

The music stopped. The quietness jolted Tim out of his reverie. He watched as Gina climbed down off the stage. As she walked by Tim he smelled the commingled odor of her sweat and perfume.

"See you tomorrow night, Ringer?"

Everyone here knew what had happened. Gina called him that the first evening he'd worked. Sighing, he watched Amber climb up on the stage.

The next evening as Tim got ready to leave for the final time Lewinsky came up to him and extended his hand. In his other he held a check. Shaking Tim's hand he said, "You did a great job for us, Tim. In my business you don't meet many honest people. I want you to put this check in your kettle this year. The only thing is I want to remain anonymous. Will you do that?"

"Sure."

Lewinsky handed it to Tim. Looking at it Tim saw the check was for twenty thousand dollars.

"Merry Christmas, Mr. Lewinsky."

"Merry Christmas, Tim."

Satan

Hank stared at the black pill sitting on the table in front of him. His stomach began to churn just thinking about taking it. Eying it from tabletop level he scrutinized the tablet. It appeared to be quite ordinary. He had repeated this performance three days in a row; and if he wanted to conduct the interview he had to buck up and do it. He reached out and picked it up. Just as the first time when he took it from Professor Gilbert, it felt hot. Why had he ever signed up for old Gilbert's class as an elective in the first place? He should have taken Art Appreciation.

After holding it for thirty minutes, he carried the tablet over to the sink, popped it in his mouth and took a huge swallow of water. The water sluiced down his gullet taking the pill along. Oh, no! The dreaded thing stuck in his throat. He started coughing and it came back up. He spit it out in his hand. What in the hell should he do? He grabbed the ends and twisted, trying to break it. Unsuccessful, he took his chef's knife and hacked at the shell. The surface remained unmarred. "Goddamned it to hell," he cried.

He shoved it back in his mouth, reached under the sink, snatched his bottle of Jack Daniels, and took a huge slug. This time it ended up in his stomach. Other then feeling heat in his belly nothing happened. He sighed and went to his bedroom. Throwing back the covers on his bed, he undressed and crawled in. Within minutes his breathing became rhythmic.

Hank came awake with a start. The rumpled bed clothes stuck to him and sweat trickled down his face. His wildly beating heart drummed in his ears, he couldn't remember his dream but it had terrorized him. He took a deep breath and shuddered. A strange odor assailed his nostrils; he'd never smelled anything like it. Repugnant, but he didn't know why. Hearing someone breathing, he turned his head. A figure loomed and he screamed.

The person moved over to the switch and flicked on the light. Hank stared at the man, his pulse pounding in his ears.

"Who the hell are you?" he demanded.

"Who do you think I am, Hank?" the man said in a deep, resonant voice.

"Satan?"

"Bingo"

"So the pill old Professor Gilbert gave me really works?"

"Beelzebub" at your service," the man said, bowing from the waist.

Two weeks ago, Hank, a forty-five year old nursing student, had arrived for his first Occult Studies class. Entering the jam-packed room, he took one of the few available front row seats, and waited for the class to begin.

After a few minutes, Professor Gilbert, a small bodied man with a large bald head, said in a high pitched voice, "Welcome to Occult 101, here you will be able to learn about and experience the supernatural. One of the requirements you have to fulfill for class credit is to have an interview with Satan."

One of the students snickered, a guy with long greasy hair and a barbed wire tattoo around his bulging bicep.

Professor Gilbert glared at him and said, "You won't be laughing when you meet him."

Jesus, I don't even know if I believe in God. I know I don't believe in the Devil Hank thought agreeing with Biceps.

During the first week of classes, he wondered how he'd conduct an interview with a fictitious being. Five days ago he'd gotten the pill from Gilbert.

"This pill will allow you meet Satan", the Professor said.

"How do I take it?" Hank asked.

"Just swallow it and see what happens."

Hank studied the stranger. He appeared to be of average height, nothing about him stood out. Even-featured with sandy colored hair and dressed in a black suit he looked like any normal Midwesterner. The only thing unusual about him was his eyes. They were bright yellow with vertical slits for pupils.

"Will you give me an interview for my class?" asked Hank in a faltering voice. He avoided Satan's eyes.

"Certainly, but you have to sell me your soul first", the Devil said. He threw back his head and laughed.

"You don't really mean that do you?" Hank's eyes widened.

"No." Lucifer grinned. "Do you believe I exist?"

"No, I don't. I'm sure this is a dream and you are a result of my overactive imagination,"

"I'll make a deal with you; if you write favorably about me and acknowledge I exist I'll save your sister Janet."

"How do I know you can do that?"

"Don't you know at one time I dwelled with YAWEH in heaven? Just because he booted me out doesn't mean I'm not powerful. In fact, you only have to look at the condition of the world to realize that I'm becoming more powerful than He is."

"Have you ever helped anyone in the past?"

"Yes, I helped all of mankind."

"When did you do that?"

"You're familiar with Genesis?"

"Yes."

"Well who offered the fruit of knowledge to Eve?"

"You did, but I thought Adam and Eve were sent out of the garden after they ate the fruit."

"Think with an open mind, you're just like God."

"What do you mean?"

"Have you considered how boring it would be to live in Eden?"

"No."

"Everyday peaceful, no conflicts or excitement, I'd go out of my gourd."

"So you considered your action helpful?"

"Yes, don't you?"

"What about sin?"

"You can't have good without evil."

"What did God think about what you did?"

"You know, He thinks it was abominable since He created man in his image."

"You will help my sister?"

"Absolutely, it will be a snap compared with challenging God."

Janet, Hank's younger sister, had been diagnosed with leukemia a year ago. So far none of the treatments her doctors had tried were successful. She would soon need blood transfusions to remain alive. His sister, a beautiful talented forty-two year old would soon be dead. Their parents had been killed in an auto accident seven years ago. Since both their parents came from small families, Janet was Hank's only close living relative. He adored his artist sister who had recently been written up in the Minneapolis Tribune as one of the areas most talented new painters.

"All I have to do is write favorably about you and state I believe in your existence?" Hank asked staring hard at Satan's face.

"That's all, Hank,"

A surge of hope raced through him. Maybe the Devil really did exist. Hank pinched himself on the forearm.

"Ouch," Hank yelled and grimaced.

"What?" asked Satan.

"Nothing," Hank said extending his hand. "Shake on it?"

The devil's grip brought tears to his eyes. He thought his hand would never be released and instead of being hot, Satan's palm felt icy. Right before Hank cried out the devil released his grip. Hank's fingers throbbed and burned.

"Shall we get started?"

It is a good thing I'm left handed Hank thought flexing his fingers.

Taking up a notebook and ball point Hank asked, "What name do you prefer people call you."

Satan winked. "The Angel of Darkness is my favorite. Don't you think it has a certain poetic ring to it?"

When he gone through all his questions, Hank set the notebook and pen aside.

"No more questions for me?"

"No more."

"Well I'll be leaving then."

"Remember about my sister, Satan."

Satan gazed at Hank and nodded; then Satan's eyes started to glow. The radio came on and Hank realized he was alone. Hank rubbed his eyes and reaching over, grabbed the notebook off the night stand and jerked it open. The entire interview was there. His hands started shaking and he flung the notebook across the room.

The piece took him three hours to type. At the next Occult class he turned it in.

"How did the interview go, Mr. Mueller?" asked Professor Gilbert.

"Fine, I didn't believe in the devil but now I'm pretty sure he's real."

"Oh he's real all right," Gilbert said smiling.

The next day Janet called him.

"A new oncology doctor wants to meet with me, Hank. Would you come along with me to the interview tomorrow?

They sat waiting in a sterile white-walled room for the doctor. They'd been called to come in here over thirty minutes ago. *Why do they always keep these rooms so cold?* thought Hank shivering.

They heard a soft knock, the door opened, and the doctor came in. Hank involuntarily shuddered. Janet took his hand and gave it a reassuring squeeze.

"Hi, I'm doctor Janssen. I understand you want to talk to me about treatment."

Hank continued to stare, Janssen had sandy colored hair and his features were even. His black slacks showed below his lab coat. Hank glanced at his eyes. They were a vivid blue. Breathing out, Hank offered his hand and said, "I'm Hank Mueller and this is my sister Janet."

Janet's health improved after she started treatment with doctor Janssen. Her red blood count steadily climbed as her energy level rose. Her natural skin color returned and she resumed painting.

"Oh, I feel so good," Janet said giving him a fierce hug. Today I go in, if they don't find any sign of leukemia I won't have to go back for six months."

During Occult 101 his cell phone rang; Hank picked it up and said, "Hello."

"Hello, Hank?"

"Yes, this is Hank, Janet?"

Hank heard sobbing, "Oh God it's back," she whispered in a faltering voice.

The leukemia ravaged Janet's body. Within two months her red count bottomed out. The day after Hank took her to the hospital, she lay cocooned in an oxygen tent, her breathing labored.

She stirred and gazed at him. Taking his hand she said, "Put your faith and trust in God. Just remember He and I love you."

"I love you too," and he squeezed her palm.

Hank let Janet's hand fall, he had to get out of the room. Out in the hall he slouched down against the wall as tears flowed down his cheeks. Hearing foot steps, he looked up and saw doctor Janssen approaching. He stood and faced him.

"My sister is very close to death. I hoped your treatment would save her"

Hank watched as Janssen's eyes changed from blue to yellow while the pupils elongated. Hank staggered back, putting his forearm in front of his face.

Janssen said, "One thing I'm sure you now realize, Hank-- I seldom keep my promises. But I can assure you I do exist."

Smiling, Satan walked away and disappeared around a corner.

Hank charged down the hall. Turning left, he stared at an empty corridor.

Falling to his knees, he clasped his hands together and began praying "Dear God, I now know that You are. It's odd, I didn't believe, but Satan showed me what a fool I am. Let Your will be done. Amen."

"I don't understand why you wanted me to paint a portrait of Dr. Janssen. It is odd how he vanished," Janet said as she watched Hank hanging the picture in his living room.

"Let's just say I want to be reminded that he helped you, he suggested that I contact another healer which I did."

The Loop

"So what have you decided, Mr. and Mrs. Williams?"

I looked at my wife, Cheryl, who smiled.

"We want to be cremated, no embalming."

Susan, the trim young blond dressed in a dark blue business suit, said, "Let me explain that option again. Upon your death you will be transported to the crematorium where your body will be washed, dressed, and placed in a coffin for your family to view. Once this is complete, your remains will be placed in a heavy duty cardboard box and then sent into the crematory. Are you both sure about your choice?"

Cheryl turned toward me and nodded. I said, "Yes, we are both sure."

We had come to this celebration of life center to prepay our funeral. As opposed to older funeral homes this facility was light and airy. They had a dining room, kitchen, and a large chapel area with floor-to-ceiling windows, which looked out into dense woods. This could be a northern Minnesota resort rather than a funeral parlor.

Susan slid the papers across the desk and indicated where we were to sign. When I picked up the pen it felt hot, and I dropped it. A chill ran up my spine, and I shuddered. Cheryl looked at me with raised eyebrows. I smiled at her, grabbed the pen, and signed my name with a flourish.

"Do you want to pay over a three-year period and have the money taken out of your bank account each month?"

Cheryl and I both responded affirmatively.

"I think you have made a wise choice; as soon as you write me out a check for $300 this contract will go into effect." Susan smiled and extended her hand. Her warm fingers closed over mine and I smiled in return. When she released her grip, sparks appeared at the end of her fingertips. I glanced at the carpet which must have generated the static electricity.

After we drove home, I decided to mow the yard. Having taken the day off, I wanted to make the most of it. The mower started on the first pull, but as I released the cord, I became lightheaded and dizzy. Perspiration beaded on my forehead and I fought throwing up. Odd, I'd just had my yearly physical and old Doc Benson rasped in his gravelly voice, "Jerry, you are in fantastic shape. I couldn't find anything wrong; your heart is strong, and the stress test indicated you tolerate strenuous exercise well. Rita said she never ran the equipment that fast before."

When I finished mowing I came into the house. I sat down at the kitchen table and, the next thing I knew, Cheryl shouted into my ear, "What is the matter?"

I stared at the red-checked pattern of the tablecloth. I must have passed out. Lifting my head up, I looked into Cheryl's eyes. "Are you tired? Maybe you should go to bed."

I laughed. "I'm all right; the heat must have gotten to me."

As I got into bed after watching the late night news, a foreboding came over me.

I awoke and stared at the ceiling light fixture. The nightmare had scared the living crap out of me. My pajamas were soaked and my face seemed seared. The crackling of flames is all I remembered. I had tried to run but my legs wouldn't move. The alarm sounded and I tried to look at the time on the radio but my head wouldn't move. Cheryl woke up and I said, "I can't move."

Cheryl's face loomed over mine. "Oh my God." Tears welled in her eyes and she jumped out of bed.

I yelled, "What is the matter?" I heard Cheryl stumbling down the hall and then a minute later I heard, "I think my husband is dead," followed by a pause then "2071 West Mulberry." Another pause and then, "Thank you."

I yelled as loud as I could, "I am not dead!"

Cheryl came back into the bedroom. The bed rocked and her face appeared. She sobbed and grabbed my hand. I tried to squeeze it but she continued sobbing.

"For Christ sakes, Cheryl, help me."

Cheryl continued blubbering. I shouted, "Son-of-a-bitch!"

Cheryl didn't respond.

What in the hell is going on here? Don't panic. Everything is all right. You are not dead. Maybe I can make her mother's picture fall off the dresser by thinking about it. I am moving it toward the edge of the dresser; it is going to fall at any second.

The doorbell rang. Cheryl wiped her eyes, and left. I heard the front door open followed by her saying, "He's in the bedroom. Follow me down the hall."

The picture crashed to the floor.

They came back into the room and Cheryl said, "I wonder how this photo fell to the floor?"

"I made it fall!" I screamed.

The face of an old man came into view. Wide set, BB sized eyes, separated by a bulbous noise, peered at me. He placed frigid fingers on my neck and his eyes lit up. "I'd say your husband died about two hours ago. His skin is cold and rigor-mortis has started."

"Get your face out of mine, you old buzzard!" I screamed. His foul breath made me sick to my stomach. "I am not dead," I wailed.

With rough fingers he reached and pulled my eyelids closed. I became bathed in darkness. *Oh God, oh God, they are getting ready to cart me off to the crematory.*

Hands grabbed my ankles and shoulders and lifted me out of bed. Then they carried me down the hall, out the front door, and strapped me on a gurney. The cart started rolling down our walk and then abruptly stopped. They slid the gurney and me into the back of a vehicle and the doors shut with a thud. After awhile the engine started and we drove off. *God Almighty, I am going to be burned alive.*

After what seemed an interminably long time, we must have arrived. The cart and I were removed and wheeled into a building where they unstrapped me and set me on a cold metal surface. I heard two women talking when they brought me in. My deliverers left and the women began stripping my pajamas off. "Hey easy does it," I shouted as they tugged and pulled, cutting the bottoms off. A rank smell hit me, I must have fouled myself. The one woman wore a heady perfume, and as she washed me, its intoxicating scent engulfed me.

"Do you think I should go out with him again?" the one washing me asked.

"I don't know, Barbara, he seems awfully self-centered to me."

"Yes he is, but so attractive and a terrific dancer."

"Forget the guy!" I shouted. "Don't you two know I am alive? Please, please help me."

After they finished they dressed me. Cheryl must have given them the blue suit I wanted to be cremated in. *Christ, is this really happening, I have to escape, but how?*

The one named Barbara brushed my hair. She parted it on the wrong side.

"This guy isn't too bad-looking. Too bad he passed away."

"Goddam it to hell, I am alive," I sobbed.

After that they put me into the coffin for family viewing time.

Cheryl came to me and kissed me lightly on the lips. I heard Jim and Sally talking quietly in the background and our two little granddaughters Nellie and Anne moving around. They were talking to each other but I couldn't hear what they were saying. Nellie, our youngest grandchild, who is five, and Anne who is eight, I love with all my heart.

"Do you want to come up and say goodbye to Grandpa, girls?"

Maybe, maybe I can get Nellie to realize I am alive.

I heard the two girls approach and Jim, my oldest son said, "Say goodbye to Grandpa, girls."

A small hand touched mine and Anne softly said, "I love you, Grandpa."

Her fingers released, and a smaller hand grasped mine.

I concentrated. "Nellie, Grandpa is alive. Don't let them burn me up."

Nellie's hand squeezed mine. "Grandpa is alive."

Cheryl said, "Yes he is. He is now in heaven with Jesus."

"No, no, Grandpa is alive. He just told me."

"Sally, maybe you better take the girls out."

"Come along, girls."

"Grandpa is alive; don't let them burn him up!" Nellie wailed in a loud voice.

I heard scuffling and then a door being shut. I screamed out as loud as I could, "Nellie is right, I am alive. Don't let them burn me up!"

After that I sobbed as Jim and Cheryl said their goodbyes. Cheryl kissed my lips. "I will be looking forward to seeing you in heaven, Jerry."

"Don't leave me," I sobbed.

Their footsteps receded and the door shut behind them. I heard people coming in and then I was lifted out of the coffin and put into a tight box. The sides pressed in on me. I moved forward and heard a door slide open. An intense heat surrounded me and roaring filled my ears. Total pain consumed me and I screamed, "No! No! No!"

The alarm woke me with a start. I stared up at the light fixture. Cheryl stretched her arms above her head and said, "We can sleep for awhile longer. Remember, we have an appointment today to meet with Susan Gilbertson at Morrison's funeral home to sign the papers. We want to be cremated without embalming, right?"

"Yes, that is what we agreed to."

I tried recalling my dream but couldn't remember anything other than it scared me to death.

Later that day at Morrison's, after Susan got through explaining the cremation without embalming option to us, she slid the papers across the desk and indicated where we were to sign. When I picked up the pen it almost singed my fingers and I dropped it. A chill raced up my spine and I grimaced. Cheryl looked at me with raised eyebrows. I smiled at her, grabbed the pen, and pressing hard, scrawled my name.

The Crossing

"Help me, help me". The alarm clock buzzed on the bedroom dresser, and he came awake with a start while the plea echoed in his mind. With consciousness came awareness that perspiration covered his entire body, his rapidly beating heart pounding against his tight chest. Only seconds before he had been driving a car. He remembered glancing down at the speedometer, the needle pointing at forty. Before looking down, he had seen white wintry fields stretching out to the horizon and felt the heater blasting him with warm air. Just then Mildred said, "Turn the alarm off and switch it over to WCCO will you?" Saying "Okay" he got out of bed. Jamming over the lever on the top of the radio, he heard the announcer say, "What year did the Beatles sing "I Want To Hold Your Hand?"

Slipping back into bed Dave thought about his dream. "Was someone in danger?"

Getting up and looking out the window, he saw snow lying in an unbroken blanket to the curb. The view made him think the time of his vivid but weird dream and the present might be the same.

Going into the bathroom he showered and afterward lathered up his face. When shaving he thought about his family. His three kids had all done well and had good jobs. Frank still single but Tom and Mary were married and last year he and Mildred had become grandparents with the birth of Tom's and Barbara's little girl. Dave thought about his parents. Orphaned at three, adopted by the Muller's after spending two months at the orphanage, aware of his deep love for his adoption parents, he still sometimes wondered about his birth parents. Whenever he had approached his mother with questions she told him,

"Your dad and I are your parents."

Dave worked as a chemist for the Fuller Adhesive Company. After arriving at work he told his colleague Stan about his night. "I had this unusual dream, Stan. It seemed so real. Do you ever dream like that?"

"Forget about it, they never mean anything. What are we going to present at the meeting on Thursday?"

During the rest of the day Dave became engrossed in his work and forgot about his dream. However, when driving home looking out the window at the snow-covered fields it came back. His chest constricted and his breathing became momentarily labored. Someone called faintly "Help me, help me."

Lying in bed, that night, tossing and turning he heard the clock in the living room strike 11:00 and then 12:00. Finally, after forcing himself to think about his little granddaughter, Jeanie, he drifted off to sleep

When he fell asleep, he found himself back in the car and saw an upcoming railroad crossing. Suddenly in his peripheral vision he spotted a freight train only fifty yards away from the warning sign. Compacted snow covered the road and as he applied the brakes the car began to skid, its rear end fish tailing. He frantically pumped the brake pedal but the car continued to slide. *Oh my God, I am not going to be able to stop.* Staring at the front of the onrushing engine he heard "Help me, help me, oh please call me."

Hearing a loud buzzing he awoke completely disoriented. His heart thumped wildly against his chest and a sodden pajama top plastered his chest. An acrid smell assailed his nostrils as he lay there forcing himself to relax. After his heart slowed to a canter he began to think about the voice. Was it a friend or neighbor? With a vague feeling of uneasiness he thought he might know the person. A chilling thought entered his mind; his own death might be imminent.

Looking over at Mildred he decided to endure her wrath and wake her up. Reaching over, he gently shook her. She said, "Leave me alone, just get up and turn the radio on." Shivering, he got out of bed and slammed over the lever so WCCO came on. A male announcer said, "Wellington windows are the best, and they are made right here in Minnesota."

Getting back into bed he said, "A dream is really bothering me. I think it is trying to tell me to call someone and warn them about a train accident. What do you think I should do?"

"Don't worry about it; just leave me alone. Can't you ever think of anyone but yourself?"

All day long Dave thought about his dream. Deciding later in the day to talk to Sharon, he walked over to her desk. A sympathetic person who always seemed interested in other people's problems Sharon certainly would not brush him off as Stan had done yesterday morning. He told her the story with hopes of finding some kind of resolution.

"That sure is some story, Dave. However, I believe dreams aren't reality and have no real meaning. I remember my sister telling me about a similar dream but nothing ever happened. Are you and Stan ready for the presentation tomorrow?"

On the way home that night Dave saw a train on the tracks which ran along the road. Looking at it caused his chest to constrict and breathing became difficult. His forehead felt hot. Tiny beads of perspiration popped out on his forehead and then formed into rivulets which began running into his eyes. Eyes stinging, he pulled off on the shoulder and watched the train until it disappeared. *I wish I knew what to do. If only I recognized the voice. At least if I warned them to be careful when crossing train tracks an accident might be prevented. Ah, it is probably silly to be thinking about this. I just hope that Stan and I do well on the presentation tomorrow; our project might suffer because I can't concentrate due to this stupid dream.*

In bed that night he lay looking at the ceiling willing himself to stay awake. After four hours, fatigue finally took over and he drifted off into a troubled sleep. Toward morning he found himself back in the sliding car. As he drew closer and closer to the track and the oncoming train he heard himself shouting "Open the goddamn door and roll out." Right then the engineer started blasting his whistle, the train rumbling louder and louder as he and it approached the crossing. The ominous black engine loomed over him and he slid onto the tracks right in front of it. Screaming, he felt the jarring impact and experienced a second of searing pain. Just then the buzzer went off.

The car and train vanished, but did he still have a beating heart? Reaching down with his left hand he grabbed his forearm and squeezed, almost bringing tears to his eyes. Realization dawned on him as he rediscovered the bed. Reaching for Mildred, his hand landed on the sheet. Dragging the tips of his fingers back across the wrinkles, he found himself drenched, his heart beating wildly, and shaking uncontrollably. Did this terrible nightmare foretell his own or some other person's death?"

All day the dream haunted him. Sitting at his desk getting ready for Stan's and his talk he had almost started crying. By closing his eyes and pressing his lips tightly together he had just managed to avoid breaking down. Light headed and slightly nauseous he admonished himself , *Get a grip on things, what's the matter anyway?*

When he and Stan gave their presentation it had gone badly angering Stan.

"What is the matter, Dave? You better get hold of yourself. Remember we are giving this presentation to the vice-president next week."

That night in spite of not remembering any of his dreams he still slept poorly. During breakfast, as he usually did, he read the paper. When reading the Metro section his eye caught a story about a man killed at a railroad crossing near Alexandria. The man was his age. Reading further he learned that the accident had occurred just south of town at a wide open crossing. The police reported a sunny and cloudless day but also said that compacted snow covered the road right up to the crossing. They did not think the accident involved any alcohol. One policeman stated, "He obviously started skidding and slid right out in front of the train."

This is really strange, from the description of the accident it happened almost exactly like my dream.

For the next couple of days he slept fitfully and felt exhausted during the day. He had even caught him self nodding off at his desk. This morning Mildred had said to him, "What is the matter, Dave? Can't you stop your feet from jerking? Because of your jerking I've slept poorly."

He decided to tell her about his dreams and the accident that he had read about. Appearing to listen attentively, Mildred only said, "Coincidences happen. What do you want for supper tonight?"

For the next few days he continued to scan the daily paper looking for any more news on the accident. He read the obituaries hoping to see one about the man who had been killed at the crossing outside of Alexandria. On the third day looking at the picture above one of the obituaries he saw himself. Staring at his own image he felt icy fingers grip his heart. He quickly read through the obituary finding out that Randy Sanderson was exactly his age, worked at the 3M Alexandria plant as a chemical engineer, and contributed heavily to his church and community. His wife Margaret, two sons, a daughter, his parents, a brother and sister, and one granddaughter survived him.

Suddenly a long suppressed memory leaped into his mind. He saw himself sitting on the floor playing tinker toys with Randy. He heard footsteps clicking across the floor and the scent of lilacs became strong. He turned and watched as a woman reached down and picked up Randy. The woman carried Randy across the room and out the door. He heard the door clicking shut behind them and saw himself getting into bed, cold, shivering, and feeling tears streaming down his cheeks. Alone, his heart aching, he crawled into bed, Randy gone; never again snuggling with him keeping them both warm. He suddenly realized why he always felt nauseous when he smelled lilacs in the spring.

Once again he focused on his picture above the obituary. He decided he must call.

After looking up the number of Randy Sanderson on the internet he got the phone and dialed the number. Picking up the phone on the other end a woman said, "Hello."

"Is this the Sanderson residence?"

"Yes, who is this?"

"I am Dave Mueller. I met your husband at a chemical convention last year. I just want to express my condolences for his untimely death."

"Thank you; we are still in shock."

"Could you tell me if Randy was adopted from the Lutheran Brotherhood orphanage in Minneapolis?"

"Yes, but why do you want to know that? Who are you? Your voice sounds so familiar."

"Again let me express my sympathies. Goodbye."

"Goodbye"

After hanging up, Dave stood with the receiver in his hand and started to cry. Later he saw himself traveling to Alexandria to meet the family of his twin brother.

Mixed-breed

Maria bent over to light her candle. Because she didn't want any of the other satanical worshipers to recognize her, she wore a wispy veil. The edge of it dipped into the lighting candle's flame and a fire tongue raced up it. Her head became a Roman candle before the head priest could throw her to the ground and cover her with a blanket.

The cadaverous priest yelled, "Someone call 911."

Maria screamed out, "No."

A short time later she heard sirens and struggled to escape, but hands held her down.

When the paramedics placed her into the ambulance, they did not check her vital signs. As the vehicle sped along, she implored them, "I don't want to go to the ER, please just take me home." She thrashed about, but they ignored her.

At the ER, bright lights greeted her and a cacophony of noise relentlessly pounded her eardrums. She flinched, shut her eyes tight, and continued to yell in a hoarse voice, "Get me out of here." The two burly paramedics wheeled her into a room, rolled her onto a bed, and pulled the curtains closed around her.

A few minutes later footsteps approached. Drenched in sweat, and nauseated she continued to yell. A cold hand touched her forearm, and a high pitched voice commanded, "Open your eyes."

Maria obeyed and abruptly stopped yelling. "Charles?"

A gaunt, pale man with bushy eyebrows, obsidian eyes, and a jagged scar that ran from his right earlobe to his mouth stared at her.

"What are you doing here?"

"I and Melissa work the night shift, you remember my bride don't you?"

Maria looked at the humongous nurse at the foot of the bed. Melissa's fat arms rested on the sheet. Her beady little eyes held a malevolent glint as a grin worked its way across her fleshy face. Maria shuddered.

"That's right, Derrick's old buddies. We were fortunate that Buster and Ethan brought you in. They're with us too."

Charles held a syringe in his hand which he plunged into the flesh of Maria's upper arm. She attempted to rise, but Charles forced her back down. Darkness rolled in from the edges of her vision.

"This should put you out until sunup. Its payback time for your betrayal of Derrick, bitch."

Raucous laughter erupted as blackness enveloped Maria.

At 6:30 AM Hector received a call from the head priest. "About an hour ago they took your mother to the ER with severe head burns." As he punched the end button and headed for the door, a chill raced through his body.

When Hector came into the hospital room he looked at his mom, turned away, and grimaced. Her once beautiful face now covered in rough, red skin, her gorgeous full lips blistered and cracked, spikes of her once lustrous blond hair stuck up in patches, long eyelashes gone. He shook her, and she stirred and opened her eyes. At least her vivid blue irises remained the same. After a few minutes they cleared, and she focused on him. She grabbed his hands, he tried pulling away, but she held him.

"Look at me."

Hector stared at his mother's ruined face. Bile rose in his throat and he swallowed and coughed. "What do you want?"

"Are we still a team?"

Hector stared at his mother's ruined lips and nodded. "You know, I'll have to be the decoy."

She squeezed his hands and attempted to smile, but it ended up grimace and she groaned. "You'll do just fine."

Hector wasn't like his petite mother. He didn't have her blond hair, his locks were black and wavy. Muscular, he stood 6 foot 4 inches with broad shoulders and a slim waist. Unlike Maria, who had the personality of a hungry lioness, he had the personality of a cunning but mellow canine. The only thing they shared were the eyes, his were a duplicate of hers, a deep lustrous indigo. But just as men were attracted to his mother, women were drawn to him.

Hector squeezed his mother's hands. "You'll have to get to enjoy women"

At that moment a beam of sunlight from the rising sun fell across the bed and his mother cowered back against her pillows, her eyes huge and rounded.

She released his hands, and stared at him. "You have to get me out of here, we need my bed."

Ignoring his rolling stomach, he leaned over and kissed his mother's cheek, aiming for the small spot not touched by flame. As he drew away, a rotting smell assailed his nostrils and he recoiled.

His mother nodded, grabbed his wrist, and shook it. "You have to hurry. We don't have much time."

A dull ache settled in his chest. He hurried out of the room, trotted down the hall, burst through the hospital exit doors, and ran across the parking lot. When he got to his pickup, he jumped in, folded himself behind the wheel, and squealed out of the lot. As he drove toward their home on the outskirts of town, the pickup skidded around the corners and once he almost lost it. He cursed and gripped the wheel until his knuckles turned white.

Their place stood on an isolated lot far back from county highway 41 which ran through the center of Dodgeville. As he neared home,

Hector recalled coming here for the first time when he was eight. His mother and him had bounced along a rough, rutted track which snaked its way through a dense oak forest. Finally they came to a clearing and saw the house.

His mother grinned and clapped her hands. "This will be perfect."

The headlights illuminated the structure, it cast long shadows and many of the windows were broken. Gnarled oak trees loomed over it and weeds grew right up to the foundation. Hector thought it could use a coat of paint. However, the swamp that bordered the back yard would be neat to explore. It would hold many animals and birds that would be easy prey. Hector licked his lips. In the city he had caught only rats and mice.

"Come on mommy, lets get your bed out of the truck."

They wrestled it into the back bedroom. They were both covered in sweat by the time they set it down. Hector dropped his end, and a splinter punctured his palm. Blood oozed out and he brought it to his mouth to suck.

His mommy grabbed his hand and brought it to her lips. She licked at the trickling stream and a dreamy expression came over her face. He looked into her eyes and shuddered, his legs weakened. His mommy dropped his hand and slapped him.

"Don't ever stare into my eyes, you hear me?"

Tears streamed down his face as he sobbed. His mommy hugged him and crooned, "I'm sorry, let me put you to bed. I want you to get at least a few hours of sleep."

Hector jumped up and down. "Will you tell me the story of how you and daddy met?"

His mother frowned. "I've told you that story a hundred times. Don't you ever get tired of hearing it?"

After she pulled the covers up under his chin, she sat down next to the bed.

"Well, I wanted to go to the Halloween ball, so I asked my girl friend Maureen to come, and we went. When we got there, I looked around and spotted your father right away since he towered over everybody. As I watched, he and his partner whirled around the floor, and as they swept by us, I caught his eye. In spite of my hot face and pounding heart, I locked my eyes on his and nodded. When the tune ended he came over and asked me to dance."

Maria saw that Hector had fallen asleep, she sighed, and began day dreaming about Cedric. They danced to every song, and when the band played the last tune he whispered in her ear. She nodded and giggled. They walked out arm in arm, and she leaned against him. As they stepped out of the dance hall, the clouds obscured the moon. Cedric suggested they stroll through the park which lay a block away. As they entered the darkened lane, the clouds parted and light from the full moon shone down. Cedric dropped her hand and gazed at the huge, bright globe with glittering eyes. Hair emerged on his face, arms, and hands as his fingernails turned into claws. He lifted his face, gazed at the moon and howled. The hair on the back of Maria's neck stood on end. and she backed away. Cedric looked at her and charged, with paws extended. Instead of running she stood her ground. As claws encircled her neck, she screamed, "No!"

Cedric stopped in his tracks and his paws fell to his side. A quizzical look came over his face as he stepped back. Maria came to him, put her arms around him, and in a husky voice said, "Make love to me, Cedric."

Dropping to all fours, she hiked up her skirt and waited. Claws raked her sides as Cedric tore off her panties. As he mounted her from behind, she glanced at the moon, screamed, and then moaned as he pushed his member deep inside her.

Cedric brought her back to his apartment and they made love once more. In the morning he asked, "Do you want to move in?"

She answered by putting her arms around him. Nibbling his right earlobe, she whispered, "Yes."

She moved in with Cedric and spent an idyllic month with him. With no job and dropping out of high school her junior year left her few options. Her parents had also kicked her out of their house. Cedric worked as a mechanic for a local auto-shop and made good money. It surprised her to learn that he enjoyed literature. He would read to her from the classics every night.

Thirty days later the moon became full. She fell asleep after they made love, and awoke with moonlight streaming through the window. She turned toward Cedric and found an empty bed, a premonitory chill passed through her and she shivered. For the rest of the night she stared at the ceiling, her senses on high alert.

Cedric didn't return by morning, so she went into the kitchen and turned on the radio. The announcer said, "A breaking story. The police reported shooting a wolf man a couple of hours ago. A local man had been stalked by this fiendish beast and had called the police on his cell phone. A marathon runner, he managed to elude this diabolic creature long enough for the police to arrive. The policeman who shot him said, "This beast took all six slugs from my 357 magnum and kept coming. My partner managed to shoot him between the eyes just before he got to me."

Maria gasped, and crumpled to the floor. When she came to she thought about her future. She didn't know how she would survive, Cedric paid the rent two months in advance, so she had a place to stay for a little while, but then after that who knew?

When three days went by past her due date, she went to a Target pharmacy and purchased a pregnancy test. Not to her surprise, the test came out positive. Tears flowed down her face, and she bit her lip.

A month later she returned to the ballroom. Her gown, a form fitting black dress with a plunging neck line clung to her body and rippled like the leaves on an aspen tree blowing in the breeze. A cloud of "Sin" perfume trailed after her, and her stiletto heels tapped out a beat as her hips swayed from side to side. Her belly still flat, she hoped to attract a man. She didn't have to worry since every man in the place followed her with his eyes as she walked across the dance floor. A tall, dark guy with glittering eyes and sensual red lips caught up to her and touched her arm. In a deep baritone he asked, "Would you care to dance?"

Shivers skittered up her back as she nodded and said "Yes."

"My name is Derrick, what is your name?"

In a breathless voice she answered, "Maria."

Derrick took her in his arms and swept her onto the dance floor. They danced the whole night and moved as one doing the Tango. As he stared into her eyes, she lost all sense of time. They mesmerized her, and she swooned in his arms. When they left the dance, he took her arm and glided her into the inky night. She found herself sitting next to him on a park bench and wondered how she got there.

His arms reached out for her. "You are so beautiful, my dear."

Closing her eyes, she leaned forward, but he missed her lips and brought his mouth against her neck. His breath chilled her skin, and then she felt two sharp pricks. She struggled, but he held her tight and said, "Ah, you are as delicious as I thought."

Maria tumbled into a deep, dark abyss. When she awoke, she found herself in a dark enclosure lying on smooth plush padding. The lid creaked open, and Derrick's face stared down at her, his visage outlined by soft candle glow.

He extended his hand and grasped hers. "Ah, my dear, I see you are awake." He helped her out of the casket and bowed.

Maria looked around and wrinkled her brow. "Where am I?"

Derrick smiled wide and exposed his fangs, "You are in my apartment."

Maria brought her hands to her mouth. "Am I a vampire?"

He nodded. "Yes, you are. I want you to meet my friends tonight. I want them to see my new virgin bride."

Derrick had introduced her to his circle of friends, all vampires.

She discovered they existed by buying blood offered on the black market.

"You see, my dear, we can't bite everyone, and anyway this is a convenient and covert way for surviving in the modern world. Would you like another glass, you look a little tired."

As they circulated around the crowded room, Derrick introduced her. They came up to a tall man talking animatedly to a very fat woman. Derrick put his hand on the man's shoulder and said, "Charles I'd like you to met my new bride."

As the man turned around, Maria could not help but stare at the jagged scar on his face.

"Maria, meet Charles, my best friend. He and Melissa have come a long way to be here. We've known each other since the Middles Ages."

A couple of months later she stood by her casket, about to climb in when Derrick said, "You look like you are gaining a little weight, my dear."

She imagined her face becoming hot and looked at the floor.

Derrick snarled, "You goddam slut, you are pregnant aren't you?"

She nodded, not looking at him.

Derrick sprang across the room, grabbed her by the hair, and hit her in the temple. Stars appeared in her eyes as she struggled to remain upright. He screamed, "Who impregnated you, bitch?"

Another blow hit her cheek and she toppled to the floor. "Please don't." Curling into a fetal position she wrapped her arms around her belly. Derrick kicked her in the back above the kidneys and she blacked out. When she regained consciousness, she lay on the cold floor next to her coffin.

The room was empty, Derrick had left and taken his casket. She glanced out the window, and saw the light in the east, she had to get in before the sun rose. Her body released embalming fluid, and it surged through her. As it took effect, she managed to pull herself upright. She groaned and bit her lip as she slipped in. As she closed the lid, the first sunbeam danced across the polished mahogany surface.

When the baby came, she named him Hector. As a single mother vampire with a bastard son, they were tolerated, but never accepted by the vampire community. Maria never returned to the ballroom again, she seethed over Derrick, and developed a loathing for all men. She got a job with Earnest, a fat vampire with hairy arms from the west coast, who owned a computer store that catered to techies. Earnest remained open 24/7, employing normal people during the day, and vampires at night. Because Maria had a high IQ, she did well and even managed to get her GED and then a BS on line in computer science. When Hector turned eight, she decided to take him to the country where he could grow up without fear of being caught.

His mother's voice faded away. Hector awoke with moonbeams shining through the window. Climbing out of bed, he padded across the floor, jumped onto the ledge, and lowered himself to the ground. His pads melted the frost as he slipped through the weeds and entered the bulrushes of the swamp. The wind carried the smell of a cotton tail rabbit to him and he salivated.

He brought the live rabbit to his mother who sank her teeth into its neck and sucked out its blood. It screeched and tried to twist out of her grip, but she continued sucking and its movements gradually weakened. His mother grimaced, and a dribble of blood leaked down her chin. "Not as good as human, but it will have to do. At least here in the country I won't have to drink mice or rat blood."

Hector laughed, "Maybe I will catch a raccoon."

His mother stuck out her tongue, but smiled. "Yuk, I am not looking forward to it."

Hector broke off his reverie as he rushed into the house to pick up his mother's coffin. He went into the back bedroom and picked it up. The cool smooth feel of polished mahogany greeted his fingers and he smiled. After he got his first job frying hamburgers, he saved up enough money to buy it for her to replace the old wooden box she slept in. The enticing smell of raw meat came back to him and he swallowed. As he raced out of the room, he stumbled, and almost lost his grip. Beads of sweat popped out on his forehead, but he managed to hang on.

On the way back to the hospital, he daydreamed about their bloody game. When his fifteenth birthday came, he already had physically matured. From his seat at the kitchen table, Hector watched his mother pace around the room, "I'm tired of drinking animal blood. I want you to go with me to the ballroom in town."

Going to her bedroom, she closed the door. When she emerged, Hector whistled. He had never seen her in that black dress. As she sashayed around the kitchen, a delectable scent trailed after her.

They had driven into town, and Maria told him to park the pickup in the gardens a couple of blocks away from the ballroom. "You remain here. I will come to get you after I enjoy dancing for awhile". The rising moon sent out moonbeams, and as Maria walked away, an eerie howl rent the night.

A couple of hours later, Hector heard his mother coming with a man. As they drew near, the man whispered in his mother's ear and she giggled. Human scent filled his nostrils and he growled.

"Yes, I'll go there with you, but first I'd like you to meet someone."

His mother grabbed the handle and opened the door. Hector leaped out and reached for him. The man screamed, pushed his mother into him, spun around, and ran. Hector caught him after one hundred yards and tackled him. The man went down hard. Hector bit the man's heel tendons and they severed with a pop. His prey sobbed and yelled while struggling to his feet. He tried running, but only shuffled. Hector watched him with a lolling tongue and shining eyes. As the prey moved away, Hector came up behind him and raked his claws down his back. Blood oozed out through the torn cloth. The man sobbed, turned, and tried to hit him, but Hector grabbed his wrist and bent it backwards until it snapped. With his other hand, Hector hit the man in the nose, and blood spurted. The prey fell to the ground. Footsteps approached and Hector turned and saw his mother coming. Her eyes glowed with an intense fire.

"You know what to do."

Hector bent down, clamped his jaws around the man's neck, and ripped his throat open. He held his head up while his mother filled her wine glass from the pulsing flow.

They attended dances every three to four months, each time during a full moon.

Hector pulled into the hospital grounds and parked in the back of the lot. The morning sun lit the building and formed a golden halo around it. When he climbed through the window he gagged. A foul odor filled the room, and his mother did not respond when he approached the bed. He wrapped her in the sheets, flung her stiff remains over his shoulder, and climbed back out the window. As he hurried across the parking lot, tears flowed down his face.

He buried her in the backyard next to the swamp. Every time of a full moon, he would capture an animal, bring it back to her grave, rip out its throat, and fill a wine glass. He would then drink it and say, "In remembrance of you."

Triathlon

Paul dipped his paddle in and shivered. He looked over to his left at the starter boat. Turning back to Brad, he said, "I hope we don't take a spill."

They sat on the right side of the pack, the nearest canoe bumped theirs, and they rocked. Paul braced against his paddle, steadying their craft. Nauseated, he glanced at his watch and his heart rate increased. Only a couple of more minutes remained. He breathed in through his nose and exhaled out his mouth. The smell of sun block wafted across the water.

"Relax, Paul, we still have at least a minute."

"What side do you want me to start on?"

"Start on the right."

They didn't want to get boxed in or end up turned over. Paul smiled; he had trained hard for this October race. He fumbled trying to zero his stopwatch and silently cursed. By the time he got it set there were only ten seconds left. Canoes edged up to the imaginary line; some looked like they were over it. He yawned as his heart rate kicked up a notch.

The man in the bow of the starter boat raised his gun. "Canoes to the line. Get set"

"*Bang!*"

Paul punched the set button on his watch and dug his paddle in. He made six quick strokes on the right. The bow swung to the left. A series of "Huts" erupted, echoing across the water. Brad yelled "Hut!" and he switched over to the other side.

A chorus of huts again came, built to a crescendo, and then tailed

off. Water thrown up by paddlers landed in some of the bunched canoes. They inched ahead to the front of the pack and Paul grinned.
He watched the bow's water line as it flowed and gurgled around the
thin skin of their Kevlar racing canoe. The thrusts from his and Brad's
paddles flexed its hull. They soon fell into a smooth rhythm. Taking a
quick look behind, he saw the other racers strung out in a wavering
line. One canoe had gone over and two heads poked up beside it. After
two hundred yards, only one canoe remained ahead of them.

Paul increased his stroke rate and shouted. "Let's catch them."

Within five minutes the other canoe was only one length ahead.
Sweat trickled down his face and stung his eyes. They inched up on the
other boat and their bow crossed over its wake. The stern man's hair
glistened and his neck glowed bright red as his muscles bulged with
each pull of his paddle. Paul gritted his teeth and bore down. They
started to move from the other's stern to its front. The competing
duo looked over and increased their stroke rate, but after a couple of
minutes they drew abreast of its bow. The pale, skinny, silver haired
bowman turned and looked at Paul with yellowish eyes. Paul became
queasy and blackness danced at the periphery of his vision.

Shadowy images appeared and slowly cleared. The interior of his
old Chevy became visible and he became aware of a winter land-
scape. He glanced out the left window, and his heart kicked into high
gear. A train engine loomed, and Paul instinctively pumped his foot.
The back end of his car fish tailed and skidded on the compacted
snow. A thought flashed through his mind that he should open the
door and roll out. The train's horn blasted as it neared the crossing
and the engineer looked down wide-eyed. They were going to col-
lide! The seat belt dug into his belly as the car slammed to an abrupt
stop. The engine thundered by, missing the hood by inches. He stared
at the small patch of bare asphalt before the crossing as the Chevy
rocked and swayed. After the train passed, he shook uncontrollably,
his heart hammering in his cold chest. Minutes passed before he

managed to turn the key and restart the car.

"Hut! Hut! Hut!"

Paul shook his head, swiveling around; he stared at Brad's crimson face, his wide open mouth, and his jerky movements. The other canoe was now ahead. Paul plunged his paddle in, and pulled. Eddies formed and swirled behind the blade as he paddled at an insane rate. .

Brad yelled, "Slow down, I can't keep up."

Paul slowed but kept his eyes riveted on the other craft. They came up on the other canoe but this time when they passed its bow, he stared straight ahead.

The hull scraped up the sand. They were the first ones in. Jumping out, he reached down and grabbed the gunwales. Brad leaped into the water and splashed ashore.

"Good luck." He slapped Brad's palms.

"Good luck to you, partner." Brad grinned and trotted toward the asphalt trail.

Paul started up the beach after him and stumbled. His legs were stiff tree trunks and needles poked into his calves as he pounded up the sand toward the running path, his gait jerky. His grimace turned into a smile as the crowd clapped and yelled.

"Way to go."

"Great canoe leg."

"You guys are in first place."

Clasping his hands, he waved them above his head.

He studied the faces as he went by, looking for his wife Betty and their infant son Jim, but he didn't see them, his stomach began a slow roll.

He started down the asphalt path. Lake Harriet, the lake they had canoed on, lay next to Calhoun Lake, which had a five mile loop. The pre-race plan he had formulated was to keep Brad in sight. His friend, lean with supple muscles and a smooth running style, always beat him in the run segment. When they got on their bikes, Paul would catch him. As his feet contacted the blacktop, small jolts of pain shot up his legs, but after a hundred yards he settled into a rhythm and his stride smoothed. Brad was only a few yards ahead and an adrenaline wave surged through his body.

Brad had gained a couple hundred yards by the halfway point. He looked at his watch and grinned. Coming up to the water stop, he saw a pale, lanky, silver haired man drinking and his eyes widened. The man turned around and smiled, holding out the cup of water, his bluish lips vivid against his white dry skin. His yellowish eyes glittered under bushy eyebrows and for an instant Paul thought they became opaque. Shuddering as he reached for the cup, his vision darkened and he staggered. Paul reached to grab the rest stop's table edge, the metal cold on his finger tips. Instead of being sharp-edged it turned round and he wrapped his fingers around it. Paul stared at a hanging bag, he held onto an IV stand. The bag was almost empty, and bubbles rose in the yellow liquid, as it dripped into the tube leading to the needle stuck in his vein. A hospital smell washed over him and he shuddered, disturbing the needle. The metal seemed to swell and the back of his hand burned.

The door opened with a whoosh and Dr. Rickert, a man with a large bald head and ears, stepped in. Smiling he said, "Good news, Paul. When we removed the tumor we got most of it and the chemotherapy has done its job. There is no sign of cancer. You'll only have to endure a few more treatments, but your prognosis is excellent."

Someone shook his shoulder.

"Are you all right mister? Do you want to continue?"

Paul shook his head. Down on one knee, his face rested against the table edge, his vision slowly cleared. The empty cup lay on the path with a long tongue of water running away from it.

"I'm alright. I felt a little faint. Give me a cup of water."

The stocky, dark haired girl with the tight tee shirt handed him one. Out of the corner of his eye, he saw two runners go past. He gulped and coughed. Some of the water dribbled down his chin as he shakily got to his feet. Three more runners went by. Paul threw the cardboard cup and started running.

By the time he got to the bike corral he had passed four of the runners and he saw the fifth sitting in the corral taking his running shoes off. Paul ran past him down the lanes looking for his bike.

A railroad track appeared between his eyes, and he glanced from side to side as he ran down the aisle. The track disappeared when he spotted it. He sat down and jerked off his running shoes, jammed on his bike shoes, pulled on his gloves, and set his helmet on his head. The buckle refused to clasp and he cursed. After losing precious seconds, he heard a click. Grabbing his bike, he ran to the exit. Many people crowded up against the ropes as he hopped on his bike.

"Way to go"

"There are only two guys ahead of you."

"Great job, go get them."

Paul looked for his wife Betty, his son Jim, and his daughter-in-law Renee but failed to spot them. A chill raced up his spine and ended up tightening his scalp.

As he rode, the wind cooled him and he grinned while maintaining an easy spin. Staring ahead, he saw the last runner who had passed him. The guy had a seventy yard lead, but Paul increased his cadence and began coming up on him. With his rear wheel inches from the guy's front tire, he swung out from behind the others bike causing his bike to lean inward and then outward as he blew by the other racer.

They had to make eight laps around the lake so he had plenty of time to catch Brad. On the fourth lap he spotted his neon blue singlet. His knuckles whitened as he pushed and pulled the pedals, concentrating on maintaining power. Calf muscles bulging, he accelerated, and at the end of the lap Brad's lead had shrunk to fifty yards. Brad glanced back and saw Paul approaching. Snapping his head around, Brad increased his pedal rate, his muscles standing out with the effort. For awhile the space between them remained constant, but then Paul began inching up. At the start of the fifth lap he caught him and swept by Brad, he had the lead! Glancing down at his computer, he saw 28 mph and he laughed. When he passed the finishing area people clapped and shouted.

"Keep it up; you've got the race won."

"Only two more laps to go."

"You're looking great, keep pumping."

"You're out in front, kick butt."

Paul started the sixth lap. Looking ahead, he saw a lean, gray haired man madly pumping, his arms and legs akimbo. Someone shouted to the old guy, "Keep your lead."

Paul thought how can he be in the lead? Where did he come from? Putting his head down, he increased his tempo and slowly drew up on the other competitor. Varicose veins traced jagged paths down the man's emaciated legs and the wind whipped his scraggly hair. As Paul started around him, the man turned and stared at him with his rheumy red yellowish eyes. Age spots speckled his upper torso and face, and his attempt at a grin exposed yellowing teeth. Paul wrenched his gaze away and looked at the black surface of the road which expanded and filled his vision. Weightlessness engulfed him and he fell. Someone screamed, "Oh my God."

He saw a raging river far below and then he slammed into a hard object. An intense pain shot through his chest as the scent of pine filled his nostrils. Paul gazed upward at six white faces with wide eyes peering down at him. He lay in the crown of a pine tree that jutted out from the face of a red cliff. A roaring, white, slender, ribbon of water snaked through pines far below him. His wife Betty, his son Jim, his daughter-in-law Renee, and his grand-kids John, Sophie, and Emilee stood above him on the rocky mountain path, their mouths gaped open. He managed to croak out, "Give me a hand up."

A hand grabbed his shoulder and squeezed. His side throbbed as he looked at a fuzzy pale orb framed with curly blond hair. "Are you hurt?"

Shaking his head cleared his vision. He lay on his side on top of his bottle cage. Grass poked through his spokes. The woman reached out and helped him to his feet. Turning, he picked his bike up and saw that it was alright. The woman's eyebrows arched and she stammered, "You're not going to get back on your bike are you?"

Ignoring her, he wheeled his bike off the curb, jumped on, and winced. Wobbling, he managed to keep upright and also stay in front of Brad who gave him a thumb's up.

As he entered the finishing area, he slumped over the handlebars, sucking air. The clammy singlet stuck to his chest, his gut ached, and blood dripped down his leg. Nauseated by his rank odor he tasted bile. He hadn't caught the old man. One of the race officials, a lean red-haired man, came up to him.

"You're the first in, you've won the race."

"What about the old guy?"

The official's forehead wrinkled and he said, "There wasn't anybody else, you've won."

Paul's eyes rounded and he stared at the official. "I won?"

Nodding, the man smiled and offered his hand. Paul stayed at the finishing area until nearly everyone had finished, but he didn't see the old guy.

At the awards ceremony, when they called his name, he bounded up the three steps onto the band shell stage. A race official waited in the middle of the floor, and he came up beside him.

"You get a cup for winning. Our leader will present it to you."

From out of the wings a form shuffled from the shadows and approached them. Turning, Paul gasped. It was the old man. Smiling, the ancient geezer extended his boney blue veined hand. Liver spots covered it, and bluish colored bruises wrapped his thin wrists and arms. Paul grasped the gnarled digits and instantly became infused with warmth. The band shell dissolved and he found himself lying in a hospital bed. Looking down on him with his hand in hers was his wife Betty. Tears ran down her wrinkled, but still pretty face. She leaned forward, and brushed his lips with hers. Paul shut his eyes and everything went blank.

At his funeral Jim said in his eulogy "I loved my dad who was a strong person, a fierce competitor who gave his all. A loving father who avoided death three times during his life, but who managed to always escape; only age could defeat him in the end"

Woody

Looking through the wire of the back stop, Randy didn't see him. He yawned as his stomach started to churn.

"The game is almost ready to start."

At forty-three Randy was still playing town ball. The decision already made, this was his last year because his muscles ached after each game and he was stiff and sore in the morning. Playing was still fun, but age was catching up with him.

Del Miller, the Wildcat manager, handed the batting lineup to the umpire. With the rest of his teammates Randy ran out onto the diamond. Heading for center, he managed to turn around before the umpire yelled, "Batter up." He still didn't see Woody. The opposing team went three and out and Randy headed for the dugout. When he got there, he took his usual seat between Joe and Ed. Randy turned to Joe.

"Have you seen Woody?"

"No."

Randy's chest tightened as his heart beat quickened. Thoughts of when he was eighteen, the first year he'd played for the Wildcats, flooded his brain. There were only twenty one in his Crystal Lake senior class but the high school still managed to field an excellent ball club. Del Miller had attended the game when his team lost to Austin in the regional championship. Going two for five, Randy had their teams only RBI and made two spectacular catches in center field. On one he'd thrown out a runner trying to score from second by making a perfect throw to their catcher, who put the tag on the sliding player. They ended up losing to the much larger Austin school in ten innings, two to one. After the contest Del came up to him.

"Great game, Randy. We could use a center fielder like you. Can you play for the Wildcats this summer?"

Randy's hometown was Browns Creek, a Minnesota village nestled in the bluffs along the Mississippi river. Browns Creek had had a baseball team since 1891, sixty six years ago. The town was located at the base of Wildcat bluff; in 1868 a resident had exhumed an Indian mound on its eastern point. There were many artifacts, including skulls from a number of bobcats and cougars. When the baseball team formed they'd chosen the feline moniker. In the late 1800s the town had fifteen hundred inhabitants but with the decline of river traffic the population fell. It had three hundred and twenty seven souls when Randy grew up there.

After practicing for two weeks in June, the Wildcats started league play. Because the town was small, they usually finished near or at the bottom of the standings. In the twenties they had won the championship a couple of times with Del pitching. Throwing hard, Del used his fast ball to overpower batters. Unfortunately, after a couple of seasons, he hurt his arm and the team returned to its losing ways.

Their field was located in a low area and some years they had to postpone home games because of high water. Early in the season the outfielders were usually serenaded by spring peepers. Roy Wilkins, a farmer whose land lay just west of the ball diamond, applied cow manure in early spring. During the first couple of weeks, if the wind was westerly, the teams and fans had to endure the rank smell of wafting bovine dung.

Bob Langer was the current pitcher; a tall lanky man with a surly disposition. When he had his good stuff he was wild and when he didn't he gave up a lot of hits. They lost the first game ten to three and the second fifteen to six. After the second loss to New Elgin, an Iowa team, Randy noticed Del talking with an Indian in the bleachers. At the next practice he introduced Ray Thunderbolt.

"Ray wants to try out as a pitcher."

Ray stood shuffling his feet, grinning, looking from one player to the next. Finally speaking, "I pitched for the White Earth reservation up north."

To Randy, Thunderbolt didn't look like much, short with a substantial belly, his hair streaked with gray. He appeared to be at least forty.

Handing Ray a baseball, Del said, "Let's see what you got."

Ray took the mound and started warming up. By the seventh pitch, he was throwing with considerable heat. Kicking his leg high, he leaned far forward releasing the ball. Billy Driscoll's catcher's mitt started popping.

Del called out, "Tom see if you can hit Ray Bob take over right."

Tom was the best hitter in the league. Last season he'd batted over four hundred with seven home runs; rarely striking out he usually managed to make contact. Taking his position in the batter's box, he dug in. Del got behind the plate to call balls and strikes. Ray threw the first pitch. Tom started backing away, but the ball came in over the plate knee high. On the seventh pitch, Tom managed to finally make contact, fouling the ball off down the third base line. Two of the next three pitches were strikes. Missing all three by a large margin, Tom walked away shaking his head.

After practice, Ray walked off the field headed for home. He'd inherited his uncle's dilapidated house when he passed away. It was located four miles from town on one of the smallest reservations in the US.

When Ray left, Del signaled to Randy and the others he wanted to meet. They gathered around him in front of the dugout.

"You want to let Ray pitch for us?"

Tom said, "He's one hell of a chucker. He's the fastest I've seen and has a wicked curve ball."

Bob growled, "I ain't playing with no Goddamn, drunken Indian.

You can count me out if you let him play."

"How about the rest of you?"

Randy saw they were all in agreement.

Bob shouted, "Son of a bitch, you all are crazy."

Stalking off, Bob didn't look back.

Turning back to the others, Del said, "See you tomorrow. Benson will be a good test for our new hurler."

Ray didn't have a phone. Del drove out to his place and gave him a Wild Cat uniform.

"You can pitch for us tomorrow if you want too."

Taking Del's hand, Ray laughed. "I'll be there."

At the game, Ray had to endure the taunts coming from the Benson dugout.

"How many white men did your grandpa scalp?"

"Hey pit face; did your ma poke you with needles?"

"It's a miracle you stay sober long enough to pitch"

Ignoring them, Ray tossed a three hitter, walking only one and striking out eight.

Randy had an RBI single in the top of the ninth; they ended up winning one to nothing. With the final out the Wildcats swarmed Ray, congratulating him.

Smiling at Randy, Ray said, "Nice hit, kid. Their pitcher is pretty damn good."

Randy grinned; Ray's comment caused a warm feeling to surge through him.

The Benson game was the start of their winning streak. With Ray on the mound they were invincible.

With the games over, Ray didn't hang around. Del dropped him off at his place after away games and when they played at home he walked the tracks to his house.

After the seventh win Randy approached Ray. There were free shows in the Browns Creek school grounds on Sunday night and a lot of the players attended. The single guys brought beer and sat way in back.

"Why don't you come tonight, Ray?"

"Ya, maybe. What are they showing?"

"I don't know, but I hope it's a Laurel and Hardy."

Surprising Randy, Ray came and sat with the young bucks. Billy Driscoll offered him a beer, but he'd refused.

"Come on Ray, one isn't going to hurt you. Even Randy has a couple and he's just a kid."

Ray had just shaken his head.

Before the movie, the projectionist ran a Woody Woodpecker cartoon. After it was over, Ray surprised everyone by imitating Woody's laugh. It resounded over the school grounds, mingling with the smells of beer and popcorn.

Randy said, "Wow Ray, you sound just like Woody."

Billy Driscoll pronounced, "You just named yourself, Ray, from now on you're Woody."

They only other game they lost that summer was the next week against Springfield. They were leading one to nothing going into the bottom of the ninth. Woody uncharacteristically walked two batters with one out. The next batter lifted a high fly ball to center and as Randy caught it the two Springfield players tagged and advanced, the lead runner sliding into third beating Randy's throw. The next batter had gone to a two and two count and on his next swing he popped up. Joe Bischoff, who Woody and everyone else called Crazy because of his loony antics and shenanigans, stood at first pounding his glove, waiting for the ball. Just before the ball plopped into his mitt, he turned around and tried catching it in his back pocket. Bouncing off his rear, the ball arced into the stands. The umpire ruled it a ground rule double and the two base runners scored the winning runs for Springfield.

Bounding off the mound, Woody headed for first. Joe's eyes rapidly widened and he started turning, bunching his muscles to run. When

Woody got to Joe he stuck out his hand, "Nice try, Crazy." Opening his mouth wide, Woody gave his woodpecker's laugh followed with "That's all folks."

At the end of the season they were thirteen and three. Benson lost four games so the Wildcat's had home field advantage for the championship. The game was played on the next Saturday after the league finished. As Woody took the mound, taunts issued from the Benson dugout.

In the first three innings the Benson team went three and out. The Wildcats got the lead off batter on in the first but failed to advance him, Benson getting a double play. In the bottom of the second they went three and out. Like the regular season game, this contest was shaping up as a pitching duel.

Woody, a good hitting pitcher, batted seventh. Leading off the bottom of the third inning, he waved his bat around and glared at the Benson hurler who had excellent control. He ended up hitting Woody in the side on the first pitch. Luckily, it was a glancing blow; Woody had jumped, managing to avoid a direct hit. The Benson pitcher had deliberately thrown at him. When Woody went down, Randy tried leaping out of the dugout but Crazy restrained him. Climbing out, Del ran up to his prone star.

"Are you all right, Woody?"

Woody rasped out through clenched teeth, "Ya, I'm okay."

Getting up he dusted himself off, and trotted down to first. The Benson first baseman greeted him by snarling, "Next time I'll tell my brother to throw at your head. We're going to get you, you stinking red man."

Crazy, the eighth batter, laid down a perfect sacrifice bunt advancing Woody to second. Unfortunately, Woody was stranded there and the inning ended without the Wildcats scoring.

The lead off batter for the fourth was the Benson's first baseman. Woody leaned in, took Billy's sign; reared back and threw a fast ball directly at his head. The first baseman ducked. The ball hit his bat and ricocheted downward, hitting him on his heel. Limping awkwardly, he circled around home plate, his face ugly, contorted. The umpire called time. After three quick circuits of home, the first baseman suddenly stopped. Raising the bat over his head he charged Woody, brandishing it and yelling "I'm going to scalp you."

Throwing the bat aside when he got to the mound, he grabbed Woody and started pummeling him with his fists. Woody slugged back as he and the first baseman grappled inches apart. The Benson dugout emptied as Randy and the rest of the Wildcats headed for the mound. After five minutes of kicking, gouging, yelling, wrestling and punching the umpires finally managed to separate the fighting players. Woody and the first baseman were ejected from the game. Trying to accost the plate umpire, Del got ejected too. Tom was forced to pitch and Enos Brown, who never seemed able to catch the ball, took over right. They lost the game fifteen to three.

Woody left right after he was ejected, heading for O'Dell's tavern.

When he got there, he entered the building and coming up to the bar plumped down on a stool.

"Give me double peppermint schnapps and a beer chaser, Maureen."

"Is the game over, Woody?"

"No."

Before taking down the Schnapps, Maureen set two shot glasses in front of Woody. She grabbed the liquor bottle, opened it, and poured the two glasses full. Setting it beside the two shots, she walked over to a spigot and placing a stein under it pulled the handle. Coming back to Woody, she set the beer down by the schnapps.

Woody raised the first glass with a trembling hand, spilling some liquor. He brought the glass to his lips, threw his head back and drained the tumbler. Slamming it down, he grabbed the second and downed it. In one long swallow he gulped the beer, his Adam's apple bobbing. Setting the empty stein down, he wiped foam off his mouth with the back of his hand.

"Hit me again."

This process was repeated five times. Finally Maureen said, "You've had enough, Woody. Go home."

As Woody staggered toward the door the phrase, "That's all folks" kept running through his mind. Nearly falling as he started down the railroad embankment, he high stepped over the rail at its bottom. Starting to walk on the rough ties, he stumbled and landed alongside the track. His right leg across the steel ribbon, Woody lay unconscious.

The brakes didn't stop the train in time. His eyes shut tight; the engineer didn't feel the miniscule lurch as the engine ran over the man's leg. When the train finally ground to a halt, the engineer and fireman leaped from the cab. Running back, they found Woody ashen faced, his leg cut off, blood spurting from a severed artery. The engineer unbuckled his belt, yanked it off and wrapped it around the bleeding stump. Tightening it, he managed to staunch the flow of blood. At the sound of a thud, he looked around and found his coworker lying face down alongside the track. Light headed and nauseous from the smell and gore himself, he just managed to keep from passing out.

Woody was taken by ambulance to the La Crosse hospital where they operated on his leg. After he stabilized, they evacuated him to the VA hospital at Fort Snelling.

When the game finished, Del and the team left almost immediately. They couldn't stand the Benson players celebrating. Trooping into O'Dell's, they wanted to drink a few beers and commiserate together over their loss. After they were inside Maureen cried out, "You don't know what happened to Woody?"

An icy feeling gripped Randy.

Del asked, "What?"

"Woody came here before the game ended, I didn't ask him why. He drank a lot before leaving. On his way home, he fell on the tracks and a train ran over his leg. They took him by ambulance to La Crosse."

Del blanched.

"Can I use your phone, Maureen?"

After looking up the number of the Gunderson hospital, Del dialed with a shaking hand; the bar very quiet.

Getting off the phone, Del sighed. "Woody is alive, they operated on him and he's on his way to the VA hospital in St. Paul."

A week later, Randy and Del drove up to see him.

"Did you win the game?"

"No, we lost big."

Woody laughed, "Maybe you'll win next year."

Del and Randy visited him again two months later. Woody was wearing an artificial leg composed mostly of wood.

Randy said, "Do you still want to be called, Woody, Ray?"

Woody woodpecker's laugh startled the man in the next bed. Looking over at Woody, he grinned and gave a thumb's up.

Joe gave him a shove, "You're on deck, Randy. What were you thinking so hard about?"

After the game, Del and Randy drove out to Woody's. They found him lying face down in his yard, apparently dead from a heart attack. He was wearing his old Wildcat's cap. Woody had never taken a drink after he came home from the VA hospital. Attending every game, he limped in and sat directly behind the back stop so he could watch the pitchers.

At his funeral Randy learned Woody not only was the best pitcher in Wildcat history but had been awarded the bronze and silver stars in the Korean War. He'd never mentioned anything about his military service.

Trophy

Her smell was growing much stronger; he'd catch up to her soon. His heart started beating faster in anticipation. All of a sudden he caught a whiff of sweat mingled with a sweet odor he didn't recognize, he knew he was in danger. Flaring his nostrils, he raised his head. A shot rang out and he felt a searing pain at the base of his neck. Bunching his muscles, he sprang forward, easily leaping over the downed tree in his path. Heart racing, he continued running until his breathing became labored forcing him to stop, hanging his head he saw a small drop of blood fall to the snow.

When the buck entered the clearing its head came up. What a magnificent animal, it had the biggest rack he'd ever seen. A bolt of excitement surged through his body. Raising his gun, he sighted down the barrel, putting the red dot of the front sight just behind the animal's front shoulder. He started tightening his grip on the trigger. All of a sudden he fell, he finished pulling the trigger, but he had jerked the barrel up just as the gun went off.

He came to with a start. He was lying on his back in the snow looking up at the vivid blue sky. Momentarily disoriented, he lay there for a short while. *Damn, the stand must have given way.* Wincing as he tried to sit up, his right leg throbbed with pain.

Man what a huge buck; it would have easily won the contest at work. I remember shooting the gun. I probably missed him but I'll never know.

He had found the old stand perched in the crouch of an old twisted oak over a heavily used buck trail. Looking at it, he saw the boards of the platform were rotted and covered with green moss but he crawled up into it anyway because of all the sign. Jerry Gilbert had arrived in Two Harbors, Minnesota the night before. He was going to be hunting about twenty miles west of there on the property of a friend. It was an isolated area, heavily wooded, with very few houses or cabins. In spite of this he planned to hunt alone.

Jerry was fifty-five years old and in excellent shape, six feet tall with a lean muscular frame. After graduating from college, he had met and married his wife Sharon. They had moved to St. Paul when he had gotten a job as a nurse at the Fort Snelling VA hospital.

Recently he had become interested in deer hunting and had taken up black powder shooting. The Minnesota black powder season was in early December and there were only about ten thousand hunters who spread out over the entire state. Because of his job, he had quite a bit of free time. Of all his recreational activities he enjoyed hunting the best. Sharon had learned to accept his time away and realized that he would be gone quite a few days during every season. Many times he went by himself, even though Sharon admonished him about it. In fact they had argued about this current trip. When he had told her he was going to go hunting on Ron's property she asked, "You aren't going by yourself are you?"

"Sure, you know I enjoy hunting alone because I can do it the way I want to."

"Maybe Paul would like to go with you. Why don't you ask him?"

"Ya, maybe I will."

He knew he lied; he had no intention of asking someone else. Ron had told him about a huge buck roaming his land, and since Ron was not a hunter he told Jerry he could hunt his property.

He finally managed to bring himself to a sitting position. Beads of sweat had broken out on his forehead from the exertion and pain. Looking at his watch, he saw it was already late in the afternoon. An hour from now it would be dark and he was two miles into the woods.

Goddamn, if only I'd gotten the buck.

He spotted his gun lying a short distance away. Reaching for it, he grabbed it thinking maybe he could use it for a crutch. Putting it under his shoulder, he tried raising himself. With a tremendous effort, he managed to come erect but almost passed out. He wiggled the toes on his right foot, but because of the pain he thought maybe he had broken a bone. Stepping forward, he lost his balance, landing face down in the snow, his forehead glancing off a hidden rock. A sharp pain throbbed just above his right eyebrow. He pulled his glove off and gently felt along his forehead just above his eye. Looking at his hand, he saw a small amount of blood on his fingers. It apparently wasn't too bad. It was fortunate he missed falling directly on the rock. The foot deep snow had helped cushion his fall.

Great, I finally manage to stand up and I fall flat on my face.

Coming to a kneeling position, he wiped snow away from his face. He winced as he touched the sore spot above his eye. *I have a long way to go to get back to the car. I guess I'll have to crawl. Sharon was right when she suggested that I invite Paul along. Paul would be here right now, laughing his ass off when he found me floundering around in the snow.*

The wind had really kicked up and his tracks were beginning to fill in. A high pressure was moving in and the temperature had already fallen. Fortunately, he dressed warmly because he had anticipated staying in a stand for hours waiting for a buck. Starting out, he followed his incoming tracks. It proved extremely painful because every time he moved his right leg, pain would surge up into his brain. Feeling nauseous he just managed to keep from throwing up.

As he slowly advanced he thought about his youngest son Mark and the time they had had with him in youth wrestling. After a couple of times Mark refused to go and had hidden under his bed. Jerry had reached under the bed and dragged Mark out taking him to the gym. He told Mark, "Once you start something you don't quit. In our family no one does."

After four hundred yards he realized his trail was becoming obscured and difficult to follow.

Well, I had better get the GPS out.

He always carried it with him and plotted his course into his deer stands. It would be hard but he'd make it. With numb fingers he searched his pocket and when he felt it he wrapped his fingers around it and withdrew it. He saw a shiny purple wrapper, it wasn't his e-Trix but one of the power bars he'd stuffed in his pocket when he'd gotten out of the car. Dropping it, he began to frantically search his coat. It was gone. His heart thumped against his ribs and a band tightened it self around his chest. His trail almost obliterated,I it was growing dark, and becoming bitterly cold. He began crawling again.

Just keep moving. If I stop I'm going to freeze to death.Wait until I get home and tell Sharon she was right.We will both have a good laugh about this.

All of a sudden it became easier as he found himself going down hill. He went through a line of brush and came out onto a smooth area. Looking to his right, he saw branches sticking up out of the snow forming a continuous ridge, *Oh my God, I must be on a beaver pond. I hope the ice is thick enough to hold me.*

Just then he heard a loud crack and he plunged into water. The frigid liquid hit his chest like a sledgehammer, taking his breath away. It was not too deep, and he found himself mired in the bottom muck with his face under water. *Don't panic, just keep calm. I've got to get my head out.*

Struggling violently, he managed to pull his arms free. They came loose with a sucking sound; the smell of rotten eggs assailed his nostrils. Bringing himself to a kneeling position, he realized that to get back up on the ice he had to pull his legs free. He had fallen through right by the dam and he looked over at its face.

I can't believe this, if only I had listened to Sharon. I've got to get hold of a branch and pull myself out.

He Lunged ahead and managed to grasp the nearest limb. Gripping it tightly, he pulled but nothing happened. If he couldn't get out he would die right here. His arms felt leaden and he thought about just relaxing but instead he made one last ditch effort. *Please, God.*

Gritting his teeth, he pulled with all his might. When his feet broke free his right leg seemed to separate just above the ankle. He screamed and passed out.

Coming to a few minutes later, he realized that his feet were still in the water, but they were free. *Get out, otherwise you are a goner.*

Grabbing branches further ahead, he was able to pull his feet out. He lay there gasping for breath. He knew that he was in a bad way. His clothing all wet; ice already forming on them. There was only five feet of dam between him and the shore so he started to drag himself over the tangled intertwined branches. His immediate goal was to get off the dam and back up on the bank.

Suddenly he saw his two boys. They and he were sitting in their canoe and both Shane and Mark were saying, "We were not trying to throw our lures up on the bank, dad, they just happened to accidentally land there."

Sharon sat on the bank behind the canoe and said, "I will always love you Jerry, but sometimes you can be so stubborn."

If only I had listened to you. Yes, I'll take the garbage out on Monday.

Tom Janssen made his way through the brush to reach his favorite brook trout spot, a beaver dam that had always proved productive in the past. *I hope they are feeding like the last time I was here.*

Finally breaking through the brush, he came out on a hillside covered with pink Lady Slippers. He knew that all he had to do was go down the hill and through the tag alders and he would be fishing.

A short distance ahead, he saw a strange shape lying on the ground. He thought it must be a deer carcass but as he came closer he let out an involuntary gasp. A skeletal hand stuck out of a sleeve of a faded orange hunting jacket. Tom looked at the remains of Jerry's body. They had searched for Jerry the previous fall and mid way through the winter before giving up. It had snowed a lot and there were deep drifts in the woods; his body had remained well hidden.

Tom heard a snort. Looking up, he saw a huge deer bolt from the tag alders and run up the flower-covered hill.

CPSIA information can be obtained at www.ICGtesting.com
Printed in the USA
BVOW02s1715280314

349109BV00001B/62/P